THE BARISTA'S BELOVED

THE RIVER HILL SERIES

REBECCA NORINNE

JAMAILA BRINKLEY

To all the badass boss babes out there, working hard and finding love, this one's for you.

CONTENTS

ABOUT THIS BOOK

Return to River Hill, where the coffee isn't the only thing that'll leave you buzzing.

It's been months since whiskey maker Maeve Brennan has been on a date, and she's coming dangerously close to giving up on men altogether—until she crosses paths with River Hill's sexy new barista. But Ben's made it clear he only wants to be friends, so Maeve will definitely stop fantasizing about his forearms. Probably. Maybe.

Former lawyer Ben Worthington never thought he'd be living above his best friend's garage and slinging coffee, but there's a lot about his life that doesn't make sense. Like his attraction to the town's beloved distiller. But since Maeve's made it clear she doesn't have time for romance, Ben will stop dreaming about her naked. Soon. Eventually.

But when the youth center where Maeve volunteers comes under fire from a big-city developer, Ben realizes he's exactly the type of hero she needs. He just hopes she can live with his take-no-prisoners approach to winning, because he's pretty sure he can't live without her.

1

"To the last two standing!" Maeve Brennan was drunk. She must be, or she wouldn't have toasted her single-hood quite so exuberantly. Max Vergaras clinked glasses with her over the bar, but she didn't miss the wince that crossed his handsome face. She leveled a finger at him. Tried to, anyway. It wove and bobbed until it landed just to the left of his nose, poking into his cheek. "You're not any happier about it than I am."

He gently grasped her finger and removed it from his face. "Not particularly, no."

"Well, what are you doing about it?" Maeve attempted her best intimidating face. She'd grown up with three older brothers who she'd had to hold her own against, so she thought she was doing a pretty good job of it, but Max didn't seem very intimidated.

He shrugged. "It's hard for chefs to date since we have such weird schedules."

Maeve snorted. "So do bakers. And Sean and Jess just got married." Her voice trailed away on the last word. Jessica Casillas-Moore was Maeve's best friend in River Hill, her new hometown. Maeve had moved here with her brother to open up a distillery, far away from their family and the grand whiskey traditions that had ruled them for generations. She'd met Jess when the beauty blogger had started dating a friend of Iain's, and the two had hit it off immediately.

Two days ago, Jess had come back from a surprise trip to Costa Rica with an even bigger surprise: she and Sean had eloped! Which was why Maeve was huddled here at the bar at Frankie's, Max's award-winning restaurant. Ostensibly, she'd come to discuss the joint gift they were planning for the newlyweds. In reality, she'd come to drink.

"Letsh ... let's make a pact," she said. "If neither of us is married by the time we're thirty—"

"I'm thirty-five," he said dryly.

"Ugh." She shook her head slowly. "I always forget how old you are."

He rolled his eyes. "Thanks a lot, spring chicken. You should probably dry out." He poured her a glass of water and walked away to go help his staff prepare for the dinner rush.

It was good advice from a wise elder. She didn't take it, though.

Which was why, the next morning, she limped into The Hollow Bean, River Hill's best coffee shop, and ordered her coffee without even looking up over the rim of her oversized sunglasses. The sound of her own voice made her head hurt. Listening to other people was even worse. But nobody had started up a coffee delivery service here yet. She was on her own, and she had a lot to do at work today.

"Here you go." The voice sounded like sunshine. It was the first thing that hadn't set her head to pounding all morning. This time she did look up, and beheld the most beautiful man she'd ever seen. Warm brown eyes circled by thick lashes over an elegant nose that led to a square jaw dusted by a bit of stubble that somehow looked soft. It was like Captain America had personally showed up to make her drink—especially when her eyes darted downward to his chest and her gaze followed his arm as it reached out toward her. He was holding her coffee, the second most beautiful thing in her field of vision.

"Thanks," she managed to get out. Her voice barely made it beyond a rough whisper.

"Rough night, huh?" He smiled, and she was almost certain a breeze ruffled his perfect golden-brown hair. She resisted the urge to look behind her for an assistant with a fan. She wasn't on a reality show. That she knew of, anyway.

"You have no idea," she mumbled.

"Well, enjoy." He turned back to serve other customers, and she spared a moment to watch him walk away. His back was even better than his front, the little coffee shop apron strings cinching around his waist and letting his ass take center stage. It was mesmerizing. But she didn't have time to be mesmerized.

She shuffled back toward the edge of the crowded

shop, out of the way, and took her first sip, ready to savor the caffeine-tinged goodness.

It. Was. Awful.

She grabbed for a napkin and wiped her face, sure the vile brew was dribbling down her chin. Raising the cup to eye level, she stared in horror at what had once been her most reliable companion. The cup looked the same—cream cardboard, tan liner, both emblazoned with The Hollow Bean's logo. But what lurked within ...

Maeve sniffed the opening in the lid and recoiled. Whatever this was, it couldn't be called coffee.

She glanced up at the counter and bit her lip. There were three baristas working today—the morning rush was always busy. She hated conflict, but she *needed* coffee.

She watched the line move for a moment. The Hollow Bean was tucked into a tiny building in River Hill's town square in a space clearly not intended to house a coffee shop. Max had said he thought it might once have been an insurance sales office. Now, the baristas were tucked behind a slim counter, sailing around each other in a complicated coffee-making dance that was almost elegant. On the other side of the long swath of burnished marble, things were a lot less pretty. The line curved and bent its way through the space, surrounding the few tiny tables in the front area near the large glass windows. Only the bravest customers actually tried to sit down here, and Maeve wasn't one of them.

Now she carefully edged her way through the crowd to the corner of the counter, out of the way of the people shouting out their orders. The man handing over his credit card at the front of the line shot her a dirty look.

She held up her cup in silent self-defense and he rolled his eyes.

It was almost enough to make her back up and leave. She'd had enough conflict in her life—anyone who'd grown up with Cathal Brennan as a father had far more experience with it than they wanted. But where her brothers had grown up into blustery versions of their father—Iain, for the most part, was the exception, though even he could bristle with the best of them—Maeve had decided to just...be nice. She'd discovered a long time ago that people were far more inclined to do what you wanted when you smiled at them than they were when you yelled, and she'd made such a habit of being sweet and accommodating that it had become ingrained. When she'd mustered the courage to tell her family that she and Iain were moving to California, she'd thrown up both before and after the conversation.

But a whiff of the toxic brew in her cup was stronger than the faint nausea the idea of complaining roused in her. She couldn't live without coffee, and she was already too late for work to go anywhere else. She caught the eye of one of the other baristas as he stepped nearby to pour beans into the grinder.

"Excuse me." She raised her cup and put on her best apologetic face. "I'm really sorry, but could I possibly get a fresh one of these?"

He reached out an arm and snagged it with one hand while pushing buttons on the bulky metal machine with the other. He raised it to his nose and sniffed, then sighed. "Ben make this?"

"Uh, the new guy?" She recognized the other two

baristas as regulars, but she'd never seen the one who'd made her coffee before. "Yeah."

"You're the third one this morning." The other barista tossed her cup in a bin under the counter. "New guy's hit or miss. He might not work out."

Her jaw dropped. Captain America might get *fired* because she'd complained about her coffee? This was far worse than she'd imagined. She felt her stomach clenching. "Oh, don't- don't do that," she said awkwardly. "He'll get better."

The other man snorted. "We'll see. What'd you have?"

"Er, just a hazelnut latte."

He nodded, and grabbed a fresh cup from the stack. "Give me a minute." Then, to her horror, he turned. "Hey, Ben, come here!"

Maeve looked wildly around. Surely there was a rapidly opening sinkhole nearby she could leap into. No such natural disaster presented itself, and she came face-to-face with the handsome new guy once again, hoping he didn't notice that her face was rapidly reddening to match the tint of her hair. He gave her a quick smile before turning to the other barista, as though she hadn't just put his entire livelihood on the line. Her imagination was quickly providing her with images of him destitute. The stubble he currently sported would probably grow into a really attractive beard. Maybe he had a pet! It would starve! What had she done?

"Gotta remake the hazelnut latte," the other barista said, completely unaware that there was a hapless dog/cat/bunny/hamster in dire straits.

"Oh, damn," Captain America said. No, Ben. His name was Ben. "Sorry." He turned to Maeve to apologize as well. "Sorry, it's my first day." He gave her a small smile.

She held in a small moan. She was going to get a man and his dog and/or hamster fired on his first day at work, all because she couldn't hold her alcohol.

"Here," the first barista was saying. "I think you forgot to release the valve on the roaster."

"Got it." Ben watched carefully as his fellow barista swiftly prepared Maeve's drink. "Yeah, that's the only thing I did differently. Won't happen again." He took the cup and capped it, scrawling an M on it with the nearby marker. "Maeve, right?"

He pronounced it right, which was a surprise. Most people butchered Irish names. "Yeah."

"Here you go. Really sorry about that."

She reached out to take the coffee, and his fingers brushed hers as he let go. She shivered. He noticed. His smile edged sideways a little and his eyes warmed further. She could feel herself getting even redder. "Um. Thanks. Sorry for, uh, the inconvenience."

He held up a hand. "Don't apologize! You needed a new cup. I did it wrong."

She glanced at the other barista, who'd already hurried off to take care of another customer. "But if something happens—"

He chuckled. "I'm not going to lose my job over one poorly made coffee."

"He said it was three," she blurted without thinking. She didn't want him to lose his job, but surely he needed to be aware that it was a possibility. Something Jess had said the other day drifted through her mind. *Oh, for the confidence of a mediocre white man.* Charming was one thing. Entitled was another. She pressed her lips together to avoid saying anything more out loud, though.

"Every one a learning experience," Ben said. He aimed what was clearly intended to be a devastating smile at her.

She raised her eyebrows and lifted her coffee to her nose, taking a tentative sniff before she sipped. She let out a small, satisfied sigh as the warm liquid filtered through her. She looked up to see Ben still watching her, his lips parted slightly. "Thanks. I'll get out of your way now." She stepped back, and he visibly shook himself.

"It was nice to meet you, Maeve," he said. "Next time you come in, coffee's on me."

She laughed. "Who's making it?"

"Ouch." He chuckled. "Enjoy your day."

She slid away from the counter as he turned to catch the cup being handed to him by one of the other baristas. A few more sips of coffee as she headed out the door, and her hangover was definitely on the downswing.

A few minutes later, she pulled into the parking lot of Whitman's Distillery feeling significantly better than she had at the start of the day. Good coffee and and even better eye candy went a long way to easing the shock of your best friend getting married.

Not that she wasn't happy for Sean and Jess. She was just ... she didn't know what, exactly, but it felt a lot like lonely.

It might not amount to anything, but suddenly Maeve thought she might take Captain America up on his offer of coffee sometime. If nothing else, he was certainly pretty to look at.

2

"*H*ey, everyone. This is Ben Worthington. We grew up together, and he's just moved to River Hill." Max clapped Ben on the shoulder as introductions were made. When his oldest friend had promised to finally introduce him to 'the gang,' Ben had assumed they'd be doing it at Frankie's. Instead, he'd found himself meeting up with Max at someplace called The Oakwell Inn, a ramshackle old house plunked down in the middle of a picturesque vineyard. A group of people were already lounging around a fire in the courtyard behind the inn when Max led him around the corner.

Obediently, he made his way around the semi-circle, *hellos* and *nice-to-meet-yous* being exchanged until his eyes landed on the red-haired beauty from the coffee shop and he nearly tripped over the words. "Hello again." Happy to see a familiar face among Max's group of tight-knit friends, Ben smiled and leaned down to shake her hand.

Her eyes widened in surprised recognition before she leaned forward and clasped her palm against his. "Hi. Good to see you again. I'm Maeve." Her slightly lilting accent was as intriguing as it had been this morning. As she pulled away, her eyes darted to the fire pit—almost like she was unhappy to see him outside of The Hollow Bean.

Which didn't make any sense. If first impressions were anything to go by, he thought he'd done all right there. Sure, he'd had to remake her coffee, but he knew interest when he saw it, and the Irish woman's eyes— tired and bloodshot though they'd been—had sparked with it. He'd seen the way she was checking out his ass when he'd glanced back at her over his shoulder. He'd covertly returned the favor when she'd left, and enjoyed it immensely.

"You two know each other?" Noah Bradstone's suspicious gaze darted between Ben and Maeve. Ben wouldn't exactly have called Noah his friend, but they'd gotten along well enough when their paths had crossed occasionally due to their mutual friendship with Max. The successful winemaker had been a good acquaintance to have, since you never knew when you'd need to break out a hard-to-come-by cult wine to impress some corporate bigwigs. Noah had given him a good deal on a case of his Prodigy Pinot Noir a couple of years ago, and now it was virtually impossible to come by since those vines had been accidentally destroyed.

"We met—"

"Ben makes the worst cup of coffee in all of America!" Maeve blurted, her eyes going round as saucers while her hand flew up to cover her mouth. "Oh no," she whispered from behind it. "I'm so sorry. I didn't mean—"

Max laughed and muttered something that sounded suspiciously like "so I've heard" as he settled down into a vacant seat.

"It's fine." Ben shoved his hands down into the pockets of his jeans and rocked back on his heels, embarrassment washing over him.

He wasn't used to failure. Well, not until recently anyway.

All his life, Ben had been an overachiever, excelling at whatever he set his mind to. First, he'd been captain of the football team *and* high school valedictorian, before going on to graduate from both college and law school Magna Cum Laude. At the tender age of thirty-five, he'd been well on his way to making partner at one of the most prestigious law firms in San Francisco.

But then something had changed.

The problem was, while Ben understood *what* had gone wrong, he had no clue *why*. He hadn't suffered some terrible trauma that had brought on a deep, dark depression he'd been unable to overcome. No, he'd just woken up one day utterly numb to the whole world. Burned out, his therapist had explained. Apparently, she'd seen it a lot with guys like him. Unfortunately, that burnout had culminated in him offending the firm's most important client. As it turned out, telling an entitled old man with more money than sense to go fuck himself was a bonafide career killer.

So here he was, working as a barista in a town where no one knew him or how he'd gone down in an epic blaze of glory. When Max had offered him the use of the apartment over his garage, River Hill had seemed like the perfect place to lay low until he figured out his next move. Now, he wondered if that wasn't a bad idea, too. Max had assured him that his friends wouldn't give two shits about what he did for a living, but that was easy for a James Beard award winner to say. Based on Maeve's outburst, he was beginning to have his doubts.

"No, it's *not* fine," Maeve said, pulling his thoughts back to the conversation. "I was rude, and that was uncalled for. I'm sorry."

"It's cool. Don't worry about it, okay?" The sooner they could move on from this conversation, the better. Ben knew he wasn't going to win any awards for handing out coffee, and it wasn't like working as a barista was his life's ambition. Still, the idea that he couldn't do even that right stung.

"Ignore them," a voice belonging to a blonde guy sitting directly across from where Ben stood chimed in. "I can't make a decent cup of coffee to save my life, and I practically live on the stuff. I'm Sean, by the way."

A beautiful brunette dropped down into Sean's lap and twined her arms around his neck. "I *knew* you only married me for my Nespresso maker." She looked vaguely familiar. Max had said something about her having a new local TV show.

"Nah, Jess," he said, before kissing her soundly. "I married you for your abuelita's molé recipe."

Jess laughed and pushed his face away, pretending to be offended.

At the end of the row, Maeve rolled her eyes and

groaned before raising a bottle of beer to her lips and swallowing down a deep swig.

Hmm, Ben thought. She had seemed so nice when they'd met, but now he wondered if his initial impression had been wrong. Shouldn't she be happy for the newlyweds? Unless, of course, there'd been something between her and Sean. Ben didn't remember Max mentioning anything like that when he'd quickly brought him up to speed on who'd be hanging out tonight.

Jess didn't seem to mind Maeve's reaction though. "Oh, hush. You're just mad that I can't be your wingwoman anymore."

Maeve leveled her with a slitted-eyed glare. "Yes, exactly. You've abandoned me." Her face said she was pouting, but the laughter in her voice gave away her real feelings. Ben thought she might not love the idea of having to share her friend with her new husband, but she wasn't unhappy for them.

"We need to get her laid," said a tall, thin woman carrying a tray of chips and salsa as she exited the house and came onto the paved patio.

"She *totally* needs to get laid," echoed the voluptuous blonde who followed behind carrying a pitcher of what looked like margaritas.

Ben did a double take. "Wait, are you—"

The woman handed Noah the pitcher and wiped her hands on the front of her jeans. She circled the fire pit with her hand extended toward him. "Angelica Travis. Max said he was bringing an old friend by tonight. You must be Ben."

Holy shit. Max hadn't mentioned he was friends with

the Angelica Travis. Nope, he'd described her as "my buddy Noah's fiancée." If he remembered correctly, this woman owned the patio they were standing on and the bed and breakfast that went with it.

"Hi, yeah. Good to meet you." Ben hoped his voice hadn't cracked too badly. He didn't often get starstruck, but then he also hadn't met a bonafide celebrity before either.

A couple of years ago, a woman he'd been casually dating had dragged him to one of Angelica's movies—some re-telling of a Jane Austen book. Afterward, she'd complained endlessly about how fat Angelica had looked and how she'd been totally miscast in the role. Meanwhile, Ben had spent the entire movie with his eyes glued to her cleavage. While he'd admired the way she'd looked in her costume, he'd also thought the film was mediocre at best, and Angelica had done more with the material than her co-stars had. Needless to say, he and his date had parted ways without so much as a goodnight kiss. Since then, he'd occasionally caught an episode of Angelica's TV show, which featured large-scale renovations like the one she'd done here. He'd never expected to meet her, much less over drinks around a fire pit.

Angelica pumped his hand a few times and then stepped back, her eyes darting between him and Maeve. She turned to the willowy brunette. "Are you thinking what I'm thinking?"

Ben blinked at the three-sixty the conversation had taken. Max had ruefully warned him that Noah's fiancée was a bit of a busy-body, and that she might try to set him up with one of her friends. He just hadn't expected it to happen within seconds of being introduced. And he *certainly* hadn't expected her to be quite so blunt about it. Most of the women Ben had interacted with the last few years were uptight ice queens who wouldn't be caught dead discussing sex in mixed company. He thought their Botox-ed foreheads might crack if they laughed too loud —let alone guffawed the way Angelica was currently doing.

"Yes," Angelica's friend hummed, her lips lifting in a sly smile. "It's perfect. I can't believe I didn't think of it first."

Ben's eyes flicked surreptitiously to Maeve, who was burrowing down in her seat, trying to pretend she was invisible as the two other women carried on about her needing a good dicking— their words, not his. Without conscious thought, Ben's cock swelled, and he shifted on his feet to try and hide his growing arousal. Damn. He'd just met these people; they did *not* need to see him getting hard at the idea of having sex with one of them.

And what was that about, anyway? He wasn't even sure he liked Maeve.

Liar, the devil on his shoulder taunted.

Inwardly, he sighed. Okay, he was lying.

While the jury was still out on Maeve's personality, he couldn't deny that he *really* liked the way she looked. And he'd fucked plenty of women he didn't particularly like. As far as he was concerned, having sex with a beautiful woman was no hardship. Hell, hate sex could be downright hot. Briefly, he imagined ripping Maeve's clothes off, their lips locked together in battle as he backed her up against the wall of his temporary apartment over Max's garage.

The fantasy was interrupted by Maeve jumping to her feet. "Oh, no you don't!" She pointed angrily at Angelica. "Just because your meddling in Iain's love life worked out reasonably well doesn't mean I want you doing that to me." Turning to the other woman, she added, "And you! Don't make me tell my brother on you, Naomi."

The woman—Naomi—waved her hand in front of her face. "Please, like he's one to talk. We had sex within hours of meeting each other."

Max choked on his beer and Noah groaned. "You have zero filter, you know that?"

Naomi threw her head back and laughed. "That's why you all love me."

Noah muttered something under his breath that Ben couldn't make out from where he was standing. Not that he had much time to try. Maeve was calling his name.

He turned to her, careful to keep his face blank. It was obvious she was unhappy with the direction the conversation had turned, and he didn't want to add to her discomfort. He might not hate the idea of having sex with her, but he wouldn't push if she didn't feel the same. That was just basic fucking courtesy. "Ignore them," she pleaded, her eyes bright with the reflection of the fire. "They're horrible people who hate me."

Angelica dragged a chair next to Noah and settled into it. "Pshh. We love you and want you to be happy."

"And you think sex with a virtual stranger is going to make me happy?" Maeve stood facing Angelica, her hands on her hips and her feet planted shoulder-width apart.

In that moment, Ben thought she looked like an avenging fairy, her long hair flowing down her back in a cascade of fiery curls. He could practically see the steam coming out of her ears.

Fuck, he thought, *this is getting out of control.*

It was one thing to joke about sex among friends, but it was an entirely *other* thing to make one of them the butt of said jokes. The fact that they seemed not to notice that Maeve was near tears had him jumping to her defense. "Okay, that's enough. There'll be no sex between strangers tonight."

"Thank you!" Maeve exclaimed, moving to his side as if to present a united front. "I don't know why you guys can't accept that I don't need a man in my life to be happy."

Jess looked at Maeve with something that looked a lot like sympathy. "We know you don't need a man to be happy, Maeve. But you told me yourself you miss being part of a couple. Don't be mad at Naomi and Angelica. They just—"

Next to him, Maeve took a deep breath and straightened her spine, rising to her full height—all five foot two inches of it. "You want me to have sex with the hot barista? Fine." She turned to him. "Come on, Ben."

Ben tried to keep the shock from registering on his face. This was not where he'd seen this going. He looked at Max, whose bottle of beer was frozen midway to his mouth, his eyebrows raised in surprise. Ben's gaze skated across the group to see that he and Max weren't the only ones who hadn't expected Maeve's outburst. Noah's palm was slapped over his eyes, and he was shaking his head. Jess and Sean wore identical looks: their eyes were bugging out, and their jaws were somewhere down around the floor. Not surprisingly, Angelica and Naomi were smiling, although he wasn't sure they believed Maeve meant what she was saying. He wasn't sure he believed it either.

Maeve took hold of his hand. "You coming?"

He looked down at the beautiful woman asking him to go home with her, and the earlier image of him kissing her like their lives depended on it flashed through his mind again. He shrugged. "Yeah, let's go."

3

She'd dragged him halfway down the long driveway of The Oakwell Inn before she came to her senses. Maeve stopped so abruptly that Ben bumped into her. "Oh, my god." She let go of him and brought her hands to her face, feeling heat rising from her skin. "I'm not ... I didn't—"

He looped his fingers around her wrist and gently pried her hands down, though he didn't let go once her face was revealed. "It's okay. Me neither."

She blew out a breath. "I just had to get out of there."

"You're not going to see me complaining." He finally let go of her wrist and scrubbed his hand across his face. "That was…"

"Humiliating?" She loved her friends, but Angelica's tendency to meddle was like some kind of virulent disease these days.

"Like they threw a party just to embarrass us," he agreed.

She groaned. "I doubt my little outburst helped."

He chuckled. "I enjoyed it."

Would she ever stop blushing? "I hope you don't think that I—"

"No, I get it. As excuses to get out of an embarrassing situation go, you could do worse."

She laughed. "You've got a high opinion of yourself."

He grinned at her. "I'm worth it." He tucked her arm into his elbow. "You park down at the end of the drive?" She nodded, though he probably couldn't see it in the deepening shadows of evening. "Me too. I'll walk you to your car."

They chatted amiably as they strolled down the path, and Maeve exhaled waves of relief that he wasn't going to press the issue. He talked about being new in town, and then shared a few childhood stories about Max that she filed away for blackmail purposes later on. She filled him in on the people who'd been teasing her, and why—she even told him about the romance novel book club that Angelica had started.

And if that didn't put him solidly in friend territory, she thought, nothing else could.

"I'm glad I got to meet you again," she said as she unlocked her car.

"Me too."

"Even if it wasn't under the best of circumstances." She rolled her eyes. "I still can't believe they did that. Or that I reacted that way."

He nudged her shoulder with his. "You did good. Did you see their faces?"

She giggled, remembering the way Sean's eyes had nearly popped out of his head. And for all that Angelica and Naomi had been grinning, she'd seen them exchange swift glances as she dragged Ben out of the courtyard. "Surprised them, didn't I?"

"I don't think I've seen Max look so shocked since his sister told him she'd lost her virginity."

"To you?" Maeve dared to ask.

He looked horrified. "Good lord, no. I might be a d-bag, but I'm not that kind of jerk."

"A d-bag, huh?"

He laid his hand over his heart and looked at her wide-eyed. "In the flesh."

She laughed. "Well, maybe it'll be good to have a d-bag in my corner. My friends always say I'm too nice."

"I'll give you jerk lessons anytime."

After they said goodbye, Maeve slipped into her car and watched him walk down the street to his own. The view was *very* nice. Still, handsome as Ben might be, she was thankful that he'd understood that she'd been speaking out of pure rage and embarrassment back there. No matter what her rebellious body thought about his forearms or his butt, she suspected he was much better as a friend than as a boyfriend.

Especially given that he readily self-identified as a jerk.

That was enough to throw cold water on the smoldering image she'd had in the back of her mind of the two of them naked and writhing against each other. No matter how much the ache low in her belly contradicted her, she knew she was better off not following through on her reckless words by the fire.

She smiled briefly as she started up the car. He'd been almost as embarrassed as she was. At the very least, maybe she'd come out of this humiliating incident with a friend who wouldn't try to set her up with everyone she met.

Home at last, she changed into soft pajama pants and a tank top but was still too wired to sleep. The adrenaline rush from blurting out that she was going to go have sex with a stranger in front of her closest friends was taking a long time to wear off, apparently.

She pulled out her laptop and checked her email. At another friend's request, Jess had sent their group of friends a close-up of her wedding ring—something that had been in Sean's family for generations. The Amorys had run River Hill's finest bakery since the town had been founded. Sean was a fairly big deal in town, and Jess was madly in love with him even though her own family, also local, were a little dubious. Maeve was pretty sure they'd come around soon. Sean adored Jess with an intensity that sometimes shocked Maeve. Noah and Angelica, and her brother Iain and Naomi, were certainly in love, but Sean *needed* Jess.

What would it be like to be needed that way? she wondered, feeling a strange ache in her breastbone.

She shook her head. It would probably be exhausting. She didn't have time to take care of somebody else like that. She wanted to be with a man who could stand on his own, and who would appreciate that she could do the same. She'd moved to an entirely new country and started up a successful business in a field that women often didn't earn any recognition in. She was damned successful, and she knew, in time, somebody out there would appreciate that.

In the meantime...she flicked open a new browser tab and typed in 'volunteer opportunities in River Hill.' She didn't need to get laid. She needed to stay *busy*.

THE NEXT DAY, Maeve went to lunch at Frankie's. It was a standing date, as she and Max were still trying to work out the details of the wedding present they were jointly getting Sean and Jess. She braced herself for Max's judgement about what had happened last night, but he just gave her a worried glance and moved swiftly to presenting the information he'd gathered.

They were creating a joint family tree for the Amorys and the Casillas-Moores that would be brought to life by an artist Max knew on a huge piece of reclaimed wood that would fit beautifully on the wall above the sofa in the couple's living room. He was researching the Amorys, while Maeve was conspiring with Jess's grandmother to obtain more information about her family. All told, the gift would take several months to complete, but they knew Sean and Jess would love it once it was done. Currently, they'd made it through the information they'd each collected, and Maeve was halfway through her salad before Max cleared his throat.

"Nothing happened," she said without looking up from the cucumber she was chasing across her plate.

"I wasn't—"

"I'm serious." She met his eyes. "He walked me to my

car, and we chatted about how extremely awful you all are, and then I went home."

Max blew out a breath. "Okay."

She was obscurely offended at this easy acquiescence, even though she'd been grateful to have the whole embarrassing affair over with before it began. "What, I'm not good enough for your friend?"

"More the opposite, actually." He smiled wryly. "I've known Ben since we were kids. He's... probably not what you're looking for."

"I'm not looking for anything," she said. "Except a new volunteer opportunity. Look at this." She slid her phone across the smooth copper bar top, and he caught it reflexively.

"Another one?"

She frowned. "I have plenty of time. I don't overcommit." If there was one thing her father had drilled into all of his children, it was the importance of time management. Whiskey took patience.

He shook his head. "That's not what I meant."

"Just look, Max. It's a nonprofit that does mentoring for at-risk youth who are interested in entrepreneurship. They set up one-on-one interviews for the kids with local business owners."

He glanced at her phone. "They could use a new website."

"They're right in town." She plowed on. "I was thinking I could volunteer both as a mentor and in the office, help them get a little more organized. And maybe you could—"

He quirked an eyebrow. "Talk to a kid who wants to

be a chef? Anytime." Max smiled at her, and she remembered with a start how handsome he was—even if he didn't do it for her, she could appreciate sexy when she saw it.

They would never be more than friends, and she was perfectly fine with that. In fact, it was kind of nice having someone other than her brother here in River Hill looking out for her. She'd always be thankful to Max for letting Iain crash in the apartment over his garage when he'd first arrived in town.

Ben lived there now, she remembered. The thought of her new friend made her smile. A barely-passable barista wasn't going to be much help in mentoring at-risk youth, but she had a feeling he'd be supportive when she told him about it.

Wait, what? Telling him about her idea required her seeing him again.

It appeared some part of her brain had already decided that was going to happen. For coffee, of course, she quickly told herself. After all, he'd invited her, and she was going to take him up on it. Who was she to turn down free coffee?

"I just think maybe you're doing the right thing for the wrong reason," Max was saying.

She snapped back to attention, the image of Ben's muscled forearms holding a cup of coffee fading from behind her eyes. "Excuse me?"

His lips thinned as he handed her phone back. "You've volunteered at the pet shelter, the library, the tourism board, and now this."

"I like cats. And books. And River Hill." She didn't

know why she was feeling defensive. It wasn't like volunteering in her community was *wrong*.

"Do you remember when you started volunteering at the shelter?"

She shrugged. "A while ago."

"It was when your brother moved in with Naomi."

"So?"

"You started spending time at the library when your mother told you about some girl you know back home having a baby."

Maeve shifted uncomfortably. Who knew Max was paying such close attention to her life? His eye for detail apparently extended beyond his food. She had indeed started working at the library when her friend Aoife had given birth to her second baby. Not that it mattered. She was too busy to think about it, obviously. What with her work at the library and all. "So?" She couldn't think of anything else to say.

"The tourism board?"

She felt heat rising in her cheeks. "A few months ago. Angelica mentioned they needed help."

"Nice try." He leveled a finger at her. "Iain let it slip. Some old boyfriend got engaged."

She shook her head. "It doesn't matter."

"Maeve." Max blew out a sigh. "I'm not saying you're bothered by that sort of thing. You're a genuinely nice person; I know perfectly well you're really happy for all of these people."

"So what's your point?" She crossed her arms in front of her chest as though she might be able to ward off whatever attack he was preparing. A truth attack. The worst kind, honestly.

"You're using all these volunteer opportunities to distract yourself," he said firmly. "It's some kind of coping mechanism."

"For what?" She dared him to say it.

There was silence. "You know what," he said finally.

"Because I'm single, sad, and lonely in my little house?" She scowled at him and pushed her plate aside. "Listen, Mister Vergaras, I'm perfectly happy. I've got my own business, and it's well on its way to winning awards just as prestigious as yours. I'm making plenty of money, and I have more loving friends and family than anybody would know what to do with." She realized by the end that she was standing, leaning over the bar, poking her finger into his chest. "If anybody has a coping mechanism, it's you."

"Me?" He scoffed, and picked up her plate to put behind him in a bin for dirties. "Not likely."

"Keep telling yourself that, workaholic," she said as viciously as she could manage. "Seen daylight recently?"

With that parting sally, she swept out of the restaurant, leaving him blinking in surprise behind her. She had *mentoring* to do.

4

*B*en stifled a sigh as his mom regaled him with stories about his brother Nick, his sister Marjorie, and his cousin Neil's beautiful new wife. Not that he begrudged any of them their success or happiness. It was just hard to get excited when the subtle subtext of the entire conversation was that he should be doing something worthwhile, too.

Not that his mom had ever stuck to subtlety for long.

"I'm concerned about you, Ben," she said. "It's not like you to run from your troubles."

"I'm not running, Mom. I'm just taking some time to figure out what I want to do next."

"I know, honey, I just worry."

"I appreciate that, but you don't—"

"Have you given any thought to what we talked about last time? Your father and I could move the exercise equipment back down to the basement and you could move in with us."

"Mom," he groaned. "I am *not* moving back to

Portland to live with my parents." The fact that she thought this was a reasonable suggestion continued to blow his mind.

"I just think—"

"Stop. Please, just stop." Ben hated to be rude, but they'd had this conversation three times in as many weeks, and it was clear she wasn't going to let it drop without him getting firm with her. "It's not happening. Please don't bring it up again."

Through the speaker he heard her huff and then sniffle.

Shit, now she was crying. He *hated* it when she cried. He'd watched her wring her hands for years over Nick's foibles, and he hated that *he* was now their parents' problem child. They were good people who deserved to have a few years of peace and quiet where they didn't worry about either of their sons. Marjorie, of course, had been the perfect daughter—or so they believed. Just once Ben would like to fill them in on the epic parties she'd thrown back in high school when they were out of town.

"Look, I didn't mean to make you cry. I just—"

"I'm am *not* crying, Benjamin Andrew Worthington." She sniffed audibly. "Where do you get such fanciful notions?"

Rather than arguing with her, he decided to move the conversation along. The quicker the topic passed, the quicker he could get off the phone. He loved his mom, but these calls always stressed him out. It was one thing to be a disappointment to yourself, but to disappoint your biggest supporter was even worse.

"Sorry, I must have misheard. Anyway, I have to go, Mom. I'm meeting up with Max for dinner."

"Ooh," she cooed. "Send Max my love. Such a *sweet* boy."

Ben tried not to vomit. When they were kids, his mom had fussed over Max like one of her own. As an adult, that fussing had taken on an entirely different tone. It made him slightly nauseated to think that both his mother *and* his sister had an inappropriate crush on his best friend. Just last month, Marjorie had called him "a hunk of grade A prime beef." Ben had ended that call fairly quickly, too.

"I will, Mom. Bye."

"Bye, Ben. Talk to you next Sunday."

He hung up the phone and dragged his eyes back to his open laptop. His LinkedIn profile picture stared accusingly back at him. The headshot showed him with close cropped hair and a stern expression—he almost didn't recognize himself. Since walking away from corporate America—or, ahem, being *escorted* away—he'd taken an entirely new approach to his appearance. His hair was longer now, and he frequently had more scruff than not. He still wore the Oxford shirts he'd once lived in, but these days the sleeves were rolled up to his elbows and he wasn't sure he'd picked up an iron in months.

But what if his mom was right? Was it was time to stop pretending he was anything but what he was? After all, it wasn't like he knew how to be good at anything other than being a lawyer.

With a sigh of resignation, he clicked on his inbox. In seconds, the page was populated with messages from headhunters and in-house recruiters looking for someone with his particular skills and experience. Subject lines of "I heard you're a shark in the courtroom" and "Your take-no-prisoners approach is what we need" stood out, along with offers of more money than one person reasonably needed to live on.

Just thinking about the deadlines, hostile takeovers, and angry faces exhausted him. It was precisely because he'd been a shark who scented blood in the water and went in for the kill that he'd burned out in the first place. A person couldn't work eighty hours a week and still pretend he had a life. Something had to give, and unfortunately for Ben, that something had been his patience and his ability to deal with the bullshit.

Still, he couldn't lie. He'd liked the money. A lot. Especially now that he had none. Oh, he wasn't destitute or anything, but when you'd spent the majority of your savings on a gut renovation of a condo with a view of the Golden Gate Bridge that you'd had to sell less than a year later at a significant loss ... well, he definitely missed all those extra zeros in his bank account. His salary from The Hollow Bean barely covered his car payment (something he should also seriously consider selling) and, when you considered both his school loans and the mortgage on his parents' house, what remained of his savings wouldn't last long.

Which was all the more reason to seriously consider one of these jobs, right?

Unbidden, his mind drifted to Maeve, and he wondered what she would say if he told her he was thinking about going back to San Francisco. Maeve, who was the sweetest, nicest person he'd ever met, would probably stare at him in horror—especially if he ever worked up the nerve to confess the details of some of the cases he'd worked on over the years. He shook his head. No. He could never tell her about the wife of a small town grocer whose store he'd facilitated the buy-out of. Against his will, an image of the woman silently weeping in the background as her husband had signed the papers flashed through his mind and nausea twisted through his gut.

Ben slammed his laptop screen closed and dropped his head into his hands. At this point, he might as well just skip the corporate middleman and sell his soul directly to the devil.

"WHAT'S THE CRAIC?"

"The craic?" Ben didn't recognize the word, but he tried to copy Maeve's lilt as he passed her a coffee, which she accepted with only the slightest bit of hesitation.

"Whoops. Hard habit to break, I'm afraid. It just means, like, what's up, or how's it going." She paused and pursed her lips. "Come to think of it, 'craic' has a lot of meanings."

"Ah," he answered as he waited for her to take a drink. Not that he was bragging, but it was the best cappuccino he'd ever made. When she didn't immediately raise the cup to her lips, he added, "Don't worry. I did it right this time." He lifted his right hand and showed her three fingers. "Scout's honor."

She winked at him over the plastic rim as she took a sip.

Ben looked swiftly away. He and Maeve had agreed to be friends, but lately his thoughts had turned decidedly *non-friendly*. Since that first disastrous night at The Oakwell Inn, he'd run into her at Frankie's, at the farmer's market in River Hill's historic town square, and then again in line at the hardware store. The more time they'd spent chit-chatting, the more he'd realized that he genuinely liked her. Which was why he needed to curb these lustful thoughts.

Or get laid.

He didn't even want to *think* about how long it'd been since he'd been with a woman. At this point, he was pretty sure he'd qualify for Born Again Virgin status. And thinking about having sex had led him right back to thinking about it with Maeve. *Goddamnit.* He wanted to be her friend, not jump her bones. Right?

"So," he said, clearing his throat and turning back to her. "Better than last time?"

"Much," she answered before glancing back over her shoulder, presumably to make sure that she wasn't holding up the line.

That's Maeve, Ben thought. Considerate, kind, and sweet. All the things he wasn't. Also, he reminded himself, three very good reasons why they'd be a nightmare if they ever did get together. He liked his women with an edge. Harder, less vulnerable. *And yet*, he told himself with his very next breath, *maybe that was the old Ben*. Maybe the new Ben deserved someone like Maeve?

No, he'd done nothing, ever, to deserve anyone. And he'd done a lot that would drive her away.

All this internal back and forth meant he'd missed whatever it was that she was saying— and she'd noticed. A small wrinkle appeared between her fine red eyebrows. "Sorry, I didn't mean to keep you. I'll let you get back to it, then."

She moved to step out of the non-existent line, but without conscious thought, Ben's hand shot out over the counter and gripped her hand in his. They both stared down at where their skin touched until his brain caught up with his hand and he quickly snatched it away. "Sorry."

Her eyes flicked between his face, their joined hands fingers, and then back to him again. "No, that's okay."

"It's not. I shouldn't have done that."

"You didn't do anything. Not really."

They stood staring at one another for a few protracted seconds. Ben was just about to apologize again when Maeve pulled a deep breath into her lungs and said, "What time do you get off today?"

And just like that, his mind was back in the gutter.

He knew that wasn't what she was asking, so he quickly pushed those thoughts to the back of his head. "I finish up here at one. Why?"

"Well ... since we're *friends* and all, I was wondering if you wanted to get lunch?" There was the slightest emphasis on 'friends,' and he wondered if he was being reminded.

"Lunch?"

"It was just a thought. Never mind. Pretend I never mentioned it."

He stared down at the pint-sized pixie who confused the ever loving hell out of him, and smiled. Sure, he might frequently wonder what color lingerie she wore under her utilitarian uniform of jeans and black t-shirt, but they *were* friends.

Plus, he was starving.

And, if he were being honest, the idea of heading back to Max's garage apartment to spend the rest of the day alone with only his thoughts and all those recruiting emails for company was the last thing he wanted. So yes, lunch with the beautiful and sweet Maeve Brennan sounded terrific. Torture, likely, but terrific all the same.

"I know it's sacrilege to even suggest it, but I stumbled upon a taco truck out by the highway we could hit up. How does that sound?"

Maeve released a pent up gust of air and chuckled, her eyes glinting with mischief. "Max would kill you if he heard you say that."

"Yeah, he probably would. But I'm willing to risk it. What about you? Want to take a walk on the wild side with me?"

A strange look crossed her face for the briefest of moments, but then it disappeared nearly as fast as it had come on. "It's a date."

Except it wasn't, Ben quickly reminded himself. He needed to nip these wayward feelings in the bud. They weren't real. And even if they were, he would never act on them. Maeve needed someone good, someone worthy. Someone who was the exact opposite of himself.

"See you out front at one."

It was only once she'd pushed her way through the door and had stepped out onto the sidewalk that he let out the breath he'd been holding for the last thirty seconds.

Shit. He was in so much trouble.

5

"It's here! It's here!"

Maeve looked up from her logbook and grinned at Aimee Sanchez, her new production assistant and favorite employee. Not that she was supposed to play favorites, but it was hard not to. Most of the guys she'd hired liked whiskey well enough, but they came to work to do a job and left at the end of the day without thinking about it further. Aimee threw everything she had into everything she did. Maeve suspected there were a lot of promotions in her future.

Now, the tall brunette was waving a sheaf of mail at her. She'd played softball in college, Maeve knew, so it seemed wise to duck. Just in case. Aimee snorted. "I'm not throwing it at you."

"The new *Whiskey Times* is here?" Maeve stretched out her hand.

"Oh, it's here. And you're in for a surprise." When Aimee passed her the magazine, Maeve found her own face staring back up at her. She yelped. "I'm on the *cover*?"

"I thought you said it was just going to be an interview for a feature about female distillers," Aimee said accusingly. "I would have come in for the photoshoot if you'd said it was for the cover."

"I thought it was just a headshot," Maeve said, dazed. She flipped open the magazine and found the table of contents. *'Female Distillers Flying High. Maeve Brennan and the New Faces of Whiskey.'* "Holy shite," she breathed. Then she stood abruptly and strode to the door of her tiny office and shrieked her brother's name at the top of her lungs.

Iain came running from his own office down the hall, where he led their marketing and sales efforts. "What? What is it? What broke? Who's hurt?"

"Nothing, nobody." She shoved the magazine in his face, making him step backwards onto Aimee's foot.

"Ow!"

"Well, now somebody is," Maeve said. "Are you okay?"

Aimee nodded. "I'm fine. Look, Iain."

He finally looked at the magazine. "That's you." He blinked, then looked closer. "That's you? On the cover of *Whiskey Times*?" He whooped and grabbed Maeve in a bear hug, lifting her off her feet.

She laughed. "Put me down!"

He did, although he held her by the shoulders for a moment longer, shaking her slightly to emphasize his words. "This. Is. Awesome."

"So awesome," Aimee chimed in.

Maeve let the grin spread over her face. "It is pretty awesome."

"I have to go work up a press release," Iain said abruptly. "Like, now." He practically ran out of the office.

Aimee laughed. "I have to go file the rest of this mail and check on the number two still again."

Maeve nodded distractedly as the other woman left, then sank down into her chair and flipped to the page the article started on. *The fresh faces of American whiskey include Maeve Brennan, an Irish native with a decidedly new take on the classics...*

She finished the article feeling like her head was floating somewhere near the ceiling. When the magazine had called her, she'd thought it was a coup to even be asked for an interview. *Whiskey Times* was the biggest publication in the field—her father had been featured more than once. He'd never been on the cover, though.

The reporter had told her they were putting together an article about several female distillers, a growing trend in the States that she was proud to contribute to. She'd eagerly consented, thinking that Iain's promotional efforts were really paying off. She'd never dreamed of seeing her face in glossy print bigger than the thumbnail portrait they usually printed next to the biographical information about each interviewee. But there she was. Full-sized. Looking fierce and proud and competent, a red-headed child of the Brennan dynasty striking out and making waves on her own.

Her throat ached suddenly, and she wanted more than anything to call her mother. But it was late in Dublin, and Colleen Brennan was probably putting her grandbabies to bed at Fionn's house, a weekly tradition. They'd talk tomorrow. In the meantime ... she glanced at the clock. It was nearly lunchtime. And there was a friend waiting for her who she was pretty sure would be happy to hear about her accomplishment.

THE TACO TRUCK was worth the drive. Maeve felt obscurely like she was betraying Max's friendship as she inhaled the carne asada drizzled liberally with a molten tomatillo sauce that was deceptively pale green.

"These are really good," Ben mumbled around a mouthful of food. They were perched side by side on a rickety picnic table bench, facing away from the table and the other customers who were sitting on the opposite side.

Maeve nodded, and caught a drip of salsa that was trying to escape from the far end of her taco. She popped her finger into her mouth without thinking, and Ben shifted next to her. She glanced up at him, but he was looking down at his own taco. She chewed another bite and finally paused to take a breath. "Noah once started a petition to make Max keep his carnitas tacos on the menu permanently at Frankie's."

"I've had those." Ben nodded. "They're amazing."

"These are different," she said thoughtfully. "Different, but good."

"Sitting outside eating out of little foil packets is a whole separate kind of experience than the one Frankie's offers." Ben laughed. "There's room in the world for both."

"I agree, but I'm still not telling Max we came here." Maeve popped the last bite of her taco into her mouth.

"What, you think I'm tattling? I don't have a death wish." Ben handed her a napkin from the pile he'd been holding down with his thigh to keep them from blowing away.

"Do we need to swear a vow of secrecy?" She wiped her hands.

"Definitely. Might need to make up a special handshake, even." He finished his own taco and cleaned his hands. "So what's your exciting news?"

She'd texted him a message that was mostly exclamation points when she'd left the office. "You won't believe this. It's the coolest thing ever." She dug into her purse, found the magazine, and then handed it to him still folded over.

He uncurled the pages and stared. "This is you."
She nodded. "Yep."
He read the title. "*Whiskey Times*?"
"It's the biggest industry publication around. They sometimes feature a couple of distillers and do interviews. My dad's been in it a few times."

"Not on the cover, though." It was a question, but he didn't make it sound like one.

"Not on the cover," she agreed, satisfaction sweeping through her again.

His grin took her by surprise. She'd been running into him all over town, and as they'd talked about everything from their embarrassing friends to their childhoods, it had been easy to make herself forget just how attractive he was. Now, she felt her stomach twisting as a shot of pure arousal hit her straight in the pit of her belly.

She took a slow breath and returned his smile. Friends. *We're friends. He doesn't do relationships, and I don't do one-night stands, and even if I did I wouldn't want to ruin this... what is this, anyway?*

She had to train her body to think of Ben the way she thought of Max. Brotherly friendship. Her libido, unfortunately, wasn't getting the message. Why Ben's good looks did things to her insides that Max's dark handsome features didn't was beyond her.

"This is really amazing," he was saying as he flipped through the article. "You give good interview."

She swallowed, trying not to think about giving good anything. "Thanks. I'm really excited."

She watched his face as he read, enjoying the play of his mobile features. He frowned thoughtfully, chuckled once or twice, and squinted as though he were looking for something. "Hey, you don't say why you named your whiskey Whitman's."

She smiled. "It's because of a quote."

"By Walt Whitman, I have to assume."

"Good guess."

"It was a real stretch, let me tell you. What's the quote?"

She looked out at the sky, the sun glowing above them from behind a few perfect wisps of cloud. "Simplicity is the glory of expression."

"What's it mean?"

"To Walt Whitman, or to me?"

"Well, he's dead, so..."

She laughed. "Iain read it in one of his university classes and he printed it out and brought it home for me. I would stare at it as I was learning about distilling from my 'da, and think that I wanted to try something ... simpler. Every expression—that's like a product line for us—is an opportunity to refine and get better. And sometimes it felt like my family's idea of getting better was to keep on doing the same things that had worked for generations."

"So you wanted to go simple?"

"I wanted my whiskey to be beautiful in its simplicity." She remembered the long days of doing things her father's way, and the secret hours working with Iain to develop their own expression. And the fight afterward. She wasn't going to let that memory cloud her success, though. She was on the damn *cover*.

He flipped the magazine back over and stared at her picture again. "So now that you're a cover girl, what's next?"

She laughed. "Hopefully, lots of people buying whiskey."

"No modeling career?"

"Seems unlikely. I'm a little busy."

He glanced at his watch. "Oh, shit."

"Late?"

"About to be." He handed her the magazine and rose. "Thanks for inviting me to lunch, Maeve. And congratulations on the article. It's really fantastic."

"Thanks." She stood, too, suddenly unsure of what to do. How did you say goodbye to a friend you sometimes wanted to lick? A hug, maybe? She raised her arms and moved in, then realized he had one hand up and waiting. A high-five? *Oh, god.*

"Oh! I'm sorry." She moved to raise her own hand just as he was readjusting into hugging position.

"Er—"

"No, I—"

"Um—"

By the time they managed to part with a firm handshake and a pat on the back (from him, to her), Maeve was ready to crawl underneath the taco truck and die. She let him leave first so that he wouldn't see her shrivel away into nothingness. *Smooth, Maeve.*

She shook her head and made her way to her car. There was no time to dwell on that awkward exchange— she had a new volunteer program to get to.

Half an hour later, she locked her car and was actually whistling as she walked down the sidewalk to the old school building that housed Youth Mentors. When had she become a person who whistled? Well, it *had* been a damned good day, that last bit with Ben aside. She had to keep reminding herself that they were friends, and not listen to the parts of her body that wanted to throw themselves at him. Or *on* him.

She patted the side of her purse, over where the magazine lay, the boost of self-confidence it gave her driving away the last of her embarrassment. She practically skipped up the steps to the front door. While she'd emailed back and forth with the organization's founder, Joan Mayfield, several times, this was her first time actually entering the building. She was waiting to be matched with one of the kids as a mentor; in the meantime, she'd volunteered to help with some of the filing, and maybe update a few of their organizational processes.

She was looking forward to finally meeting Joan in person. What she didn't expect was to open the door of the office and find the older woman in tears.

Two tissues and a mug of tea later, Maeve had the gist: Youth Mentors and its historic building had just received a letter from a development company intending to turn the old school into trendy condos. And they didn't seem particularly interested in the well-being of a small nonprofit, or the kids it helped.

Maeve brushed her fingers across the magazine hidden in her bag, and remembered the fierce, proud woman on the cover. "We can fight this," she said. And again, louder. "Joan, we can fight this."

6

———

"Y ou working late tonight?" Ben swallowed the last of his iced tea and pushed his empty glass toward Max. It was only three o'clock, but he was bored; he didn't know how he'd make it to bed time without going insane. He'd been hoping to persuade Max to turn the restaurant over to his sous chef so they could grab some beers down at The Hut, a dive bar at the edge of town on the river.

Without looking up from what he was writing on the specials board, Max chuckled. "You could say that. I'm doing an overnight brisket for tomorrow's dinner service."

Ben groaned.

"What?" Max asked, his eyebrows pinched in concentration as he put the finishing touches on the fancy calligraphy announcing the meal.

"You were my last hope."

Max finally looked up. "For what?"

"I need to get out of that apartment, man. I'm going crazy."

Max looked at him like he'd spoken in Swahili. "So call up one of your friends."

"Dude. *You* are my only friend."

Max's chin jerked back. "Seriously? You've lived in River Hill for like six months. You should have friends crawling out of the woodwork by now. You've always been Mr. Popular."

Ben rolled his eyes. "I've lived here for *three* months. And that was the old me. I'm trying to turn over a new leaf."

"By not meeting people?"

"No," Ben answered. "By not hanging out with assholes and douchebags."

Max set down the marker and leaned back against the counter, his legs crossed at his ankles and his arms over his chest. "What about Noah?"

Ben shook his head. "He's out of town at some big wine competition. And no way am I hanging out with Angelica by myself. She frightens me."

"I get that." Max rubbed the bristles of his short, dark beard. "And you can't call up Sean to go with you to The Hut. Aside from the whole not drinking thing, Big Mitch banned him."

"What happened there?" The couple of times Ben had met Sean, he'd been pretty open about his sobriety, but no one had ever mentioned him doing anything that would have caused him to be banned from any of the town's drinking establishments, let alone a dive like The Hut. While Ben had been tossed from one or two bars in his lifetime, he couldn't imagine what you'd have to do to actually be banned from one. He imagined it had to be pretty terrible.

"Nothing." Max waved his hand in front of his face as if the incident wasn't worth discussing.

Which Ben didn't suppose it was. Lord knew he wouldn't want Max and Sean to be sitting around gossiping about *him*.

With that thought, his shoulders hunched in on themselves. "I guess that means it's Chinese takeout and reruns of *Law & Order*."

"You *have* to stop watching that show," Max said, setting to work arranging the bar for the coming dinner rush. "It only makes you depressed."

"You'd be depressed too," Ben countered, "if you went from running your own kick-ass restaurant to watching episodes of *Master Chef* to get your fix."

"Which is exactly why you need to stop watching it. You're not a lawyer anymore."

Ouch. Ben knew he hadn't meant to sound so callous, but the barb hurt just the same as if it had been intentional. He knew what he was—and what he wasn't. He didn't need his oldest friend reminding him of it.

"What about Maeve?" Max asked, apropos of nothing.

Or at least Ben assumed the question was issued out of the blue, but then he smelled her perfume. Or maybe it was the scents of the distillery clinging to her hair and clothes. Whatever it was, it made his mouth water.

She hopped up onto the stool next to him. "What about Maeve?"

Max smiled and grabbed a bottle of sparkling water

from the low fridge below the counter and then reached for a glass. When it was three-quarters of the way full, he topped it with a sprig of mint, popped in a straw, and passed it to Maeve. "You got plans tonight?"

"Nope," she said, tucking the straw between pursed lips. "Why? You wanna hang out?"

Ben looked away before she or Max could catch him staring. While he didn't necessarily consider himself a good guy, he wasn't a total asshole either. He really had to get his overactive imagination under control. Every time he saw Maeve his mind automatically jumped to all the filthy things he wanted to do to her. Like right now, he would happily give his left kidney if it meant he could have have her sweet pink lips wrapped around his cock the same way they circled that goddamn straw.

And that right there was why he'd avoided hugging her the other day. While Maeve had been unable to pry her eyes away from the horizon, he'd been unable to take his eyes off of her. She really was the most beautiful woman he'd ever met. But it went much deeper than that. He'd been proud of her, too. And seeing how proud she was of herself had been a *huge* turn-on. The first time his stomach had pitched and rolled during the conversation, he'd assumed the tacos had been off, but when it happened a few more times with no other adverse effects, he realized what it actually was.

Whether conscious or not, Maeve had shared a side of herself with him that she didn't often show the rest of the world, and the knowledge that she trusted him in that way had driven him absolutely wild. He'd always been drawn to strong women, and despite her easy disposition and obvious need to please the people around her, it was a revelation to find out the woman actually had a spine made of steel.

He'd been hard the entire afternoon.

Which was why when she'd reached out to hug him, he'd taken a step back and put his hand up for a high-five instead. Possibly offending her had seemed the safer of his options, but then things had turned a different sort of awkward between them. By the time they'd parted ways, he'd managed to convince himself their lunch date was going to be their first, last, and only one.

So the fact that Max was trying to foist him off on her now wasn't a welcome turn of events. He didn't know if he could pretend to be impartial when she eventually gave him some thinly-veiled excuse for why she was busy or how she needed to be somewhere else.

"Nuh-uh," he said, shaking his finger at Max. "I don't need you arranging my play dates for me."

"Play dates?" Maeve's voice came out as a surprised squeak, and Ben swiveled on his stool to face her. Her cheeks were flushed pink, causing her freckles to stand out even more starkly against her normally pale skin, and her eyes were wide with what looked like apprehension.

Damn, Ben thought. He really had fucked things up the other day with that high-five. Better that, he told himself, then have her feel the literal extent of his admiration. They were friends; she didn't need to know how big his dick was.

"Ben's bored," Max explained as he resumed leaning against the counter behind him. "And since I'm busy making overnight brisket, he has no one to hang out with."

"Thanks for making me sound like a loser," Ben shot back.

Max shrugged. "If it walks like a duck …"

"What did you have in mind?" Maeve asked suddenly, causing Ben's heart to kick violently in his chest. Maybe she hadn't been completely repulsed by his bumbling attempt at keeping things strictly platonic.

"I'd proposed beers down at The Hut, but—"

Maeve shuddered. "The last time I was there, Big Mitch's nephew Cooter asked what it would take to make me his 'old lady.'" She used her fingers to make air quotes. "I've watched enough episodes of *Sons of Anarchy* to know I want nothing to do with that lot. Especially since he's no Charlie Hunnam."

Ben was no Charlie Hunnam either, but with his increasingly long dirty blonde hair and the five o'clock shadow he sported more often than not, he was way closer to the actor than the large, hairy bikers he'd met the few times he'd been at The Hut. They were all good enough guys, but none of them would be winning any beauty contests anytime soon.

Briefly, Ben entertained the idea that if the scruffy, buff, blonde look was what did it for Maeve, then he might stand a chance with her after all. But as quickly as the thought popped into his head, he reminded himself it was ridiculous to get his hopes up. They'd been clear from the beginning about what this was between them— friendship, and nothing more.

It was too bad, then, that he wanted more.

"It's not The Hut," she was saying as she slid from her stool and dropped a five dollar bill on the counter, "but you're welcome to head back to the distillery with me. I could give you a tour and let you taste the some of the stuff my dad sent to tide us over until our first whiskey properly matured."

"I don't want to put you out," Ben answered.

She shook her head and smiled at him. "It's no trouble, really. It'll give me a chance to practice the messaging Iain's been trying to drill into my head since that article came out."

"What was wrong with the article?" He slid off his own stool and pulled out his wallet to pay Max for the food and drinks he'd had.

Before Maeve could answer, Max held up his hand. "What did I tell you? Your money's no good here."

Ben sighed and pushed the money across the copper bar top. "And I told you I'm no charity case."

Max scoffed. "You think that's what's going on here?"

"Isn't it?" He widened his stance and crossed his arms over his chest.

"Dude. Put your fucking money away." Max pushed the bills back across the counter. "Your mom fed Isabella and me more times than I could count when we were growing up. If anything, I still owe you."

Ben didn't buy that line of reasoning for one second, but he didn't want to draw any further attention to his diminished financial state either. Maeve didn't need to know his salary from The Hollow Bean couldn't cover even his most basic needs. Sheepishly, he settled the cash back inside his wallet and turned to her. "You were saying?"

She stared at him like he'd sprouted two heads.

"About messaging?" he reminded her.

She shook her head. "Oh, right! Apparently I talked a lot about distilling processes and maturation and all this other industry stuff without ever really plugging the distillery itself."

Ben waved to Max as he followed Maeve out of the restaurant, blinking when they stepped out into the harsh sunlight of mid-day. He tugged his sunglasses from the neck of his t-shirt and settled them over his eyes. "I'm no expert, but it didn't feel that way to me."

She shrugged and rocked back on her heels. "Marketing is Iain's thing, so he's more sensitive to it than I am. I'm still shocked they chose to put me on the cover out of all the other badass female distillers they spoke with."

Reflexively, Ben reached out to take her hand. Squeezing it, he said, "I'm not. And it's probably because you *didn't* drone on and on about Whitman's that you made the cover. They wanted to profile the people—not the product. You done good, kid." He should have dropped his hold on her, but he couldn't bring himself to do it. Idly, he rubbed a path over the back of her hand with the pad of his thumb.

She rolled her bottom lip between her teeth, and her breathing grew ragged.

Ben took a step closer, just aching to tug her into his arms and taste that lip. But he couldn't, so he stepped back and dropped her hand. "Anyhow, that's just my opinion." He focused his gaze over her shoulder instead of on her flushed, beautiful face. A beat of silence descended, and he didn't know how to fill it. He was just about to turn and walk away—creating yet another awkward goodbye—when she sighed, pulling his attention back to her.

"So, about that tour?" she asked, her earnest gaze hopeful. She was a better friend than he was, it seemed. All he could think about was getting into her pants, but she was still willing to spend time entertaining him to keep him from being alone and bored.

It was probably a bad idea to spend any more time with Maeve today. He was already feeling confused about his burgeoning emotions and how to handle them. There was an increasingly real possibility that he'd do something he'd regret later—like pull her into his arms and ruin their friendship. But somehow, he still found himself saying, "Lead the way."

***

BEN WOKE to the sound of glasses clinking somewhere off in the distance. He rose blearily up onto his elbows to try and get his bearings. From what he could tell, it was late. Very late. Across the small two-room apartment, Max was in the kitchenette mixing up something in a pitcher.

"What are you doing here?" he asked, tossing his legs over the side of the couch and sitting up with a groan. He really was way too old—and tall—to be sleeping on this small thing.

"Making sure you're not hungover tomorrow."

He pushed up off the sofa and made his way to Max's side in a few uneven strides, sniffing the air. "With more booze?"

"Just a shot. It's mostly tomato juice and tabasco. In my experience, this'll either sober you right up or have you puking your guts out. Either way, you'll wake up in the morning right as rain."

Ben accepted the glass with some amount of trepidation. He didn't feel particularly drunk, but he had an early shift at the coffee shop and he couldn't afford to show up the worse for wear. He lifted the glass to his mouth and swallowed down Max's homemade hangover remedy with a few deep swallows.

"What happened?" he asked, setting the empty glass down onto the butcher block counter. As he did, he caught sight of his legs. Legs, he was pretty sure, that had been covered in denim a few hours earlier.

"How much do you remember?"

Ben combed through his memories. There'd been that moment just outside of Frankie's when he'd wanted so badly to kiss Maeve that he thought he might die of longing. Then they'd gone back to the distillery where she'd given him a tour. Afterward, she'd opened a few bottles of gin and had given him a lesson in how to properly identify which botanicals she'd used. And then, somehow, they'd moved on to pounding shots. She'd warned him it was a bad idea, but it seemed Ben was all about bad ideas these days.

"I'm an idiot," he observed, stabbing his fingers into his hair and making his way back to the sofa. "What kind of a moron challenges a whiskey maker to shots?"

Max chuckled and plopped down across from him on the single chair the room could hold. "Apparently one who was trying to impress said whiskey maker." He paused and caught Ben's eye. "Maeve mentioned you being very adamant about that."

"Impressing her?"

Max nodded, and his gaze turned speculative. "Apparently, you thought it was important to prove that you had redeeming qualities since you suck at making coffee."

Ben groaned again and dropped his head back against the sofa cushion. Of course he'd said that.

Max coughed, and Ben brought his face forward again. "You might have also said you'd be happy to show her your other redeeming qualities—if you get my drift."

"No."

Max nodded. "That's when she called me to come get your sorry ass. Said you were talking crazy, and she thought maybe she'd poisoned you."

He remained silent, even though he knew Max was looking for some sort of answer to that. But what could he say?

"What are you doing, man?" Max's voice was kind, but there was an underlying hardness to his question too.

Ben leaned forward and rested his elbows on his thighs, dropping his face into his open palms. After a few long seconds where he tried to figure out how to explain what he was feeling, he rolled his head to the side and angled a beseeching glance his friend's way. He knew Max cared for Maeve like a little sister, and Ben sometimes wondered if he wasn't trying to work through some of the guilt he felt for not doing enough for Isabella. But that was a problem for another day.

"I've got it bad, man."

Max nodded again. "I kind of figured. You looked like you wanted to puke when she came into the restaurant. I've only ever seen that look once before—the day Noah realized he didn't actually hate Angelica."

Ben pushed to his feet and paced the room. "It doesn't matter, though." He came to the wall and turned. "I have nothing to offer her." He hated the flatness in his voice. It reminded him too much of the empty days after he'd been fired, when he'd struggled through numbness to figure out what to do next with his life. Unfortunately, he still didn't really know. He couldn't imagine a future for himself, let alone one where Maeve might be in it. Successful, sweet, perfect Maeve.

Max opened his mouth to speak and then abruptly closed it. Opened it again. "Look, I'm not going to tell you what to do. All I'll say is be careful there."

Ben halted his pacing. "I'm trying."

"Try harder." With that not-too-subtle reminder, he stood and brushed past Ben, clasping him on the shoulder as he went. "She's not someone you mess around with. Maeve's a forever kind of girl."

"I know," Ben said as his friend made his way to the door.

Then again, once he'd gone: "I know."

7

$\mathcal{M}$aeve stared at the notepad in front of her. It was covered with scratched out notes and half-formed ideas. She scrubbed a hand over her face and groaned. She'd planned to dedicate this morning to working out a plan to help Youth Mentors, but drinking Ben under the table last night wasn't exactly the best preparation. She was glad she'd called Max when Ben had glanced up at her from under those thick dark blonde eyelashes and a slow, sexy grin slipped across his face. Loose-limbed from the alcohol they'd been drinking, he'd been more than appealing when with a wink he'd asked if she'd like to take their conversation horizontal.

And oh, god, had she wanted to.

Certain parts of her body were still screaming about the fact that she hadn't taken him up on the offer. A round with her vibrator after she'd sent Ben home hadn't done much to take the edge off. And a second round this morning had only reminded her just how long it had been since she'd been with an actual, live human man. And just how big Ben's hands were. She'd pictured them on her as she'd come, biting her lip to avoid whispering his name out loud.

She was a mess.

And now she was trying to figure out how to save a nonprofit while her entire body screamed at her to pick up the phone and call Ben. Except he'd been drunk, and he hadn't quite seemed... himself. Not the pleasant, easy friend she'd come to know. More intense, and hard-edged. He'd once told her a few things about his life as a hotshot corporate type before he'd come to River Hill, and now she wondered if it was *that* Ben she'd gotten a glimpse of. He never seemed particularly proud of his past, and she remembered again that he'd told her that he was a d-bag the second time they'd met.

Sleeping with a drunk douche wasn't quite Maeve's style, no matter how many cobwebs she was brushing out of her unused lady parts these days. She liked her friendship with Ben, and sex was pretty much guaranteed to ruin it. She'd much rather have the guy who'd been thrilled about her success as a friend than one night of incredibly hot sex with the guy who wouldn't call her afterwards. *Right*?

She rested her chin on her open palm and stared down at her notes again. Thinking about Ben wasn't solving her problems. She sighed. There was only one person she could think of who was mean enough to give her advice on how to fight fire with fire. She picked up her phone and dialed the international number, waiting the standard two rings before it was answered with a brusque greeting.

"Hello, Dad."

"Hello, Maevey." Cathal Brennan was the only person who called her that. She rolled her eyes.

"I have a question for you."

"Well, I didn't think you were calling just to say hello to your old dad." He snorted. "You'd better call your mother after this. If she hears you talked to me and not her, neither one of us will hear the end of it."

Maeve laughed. "She's next on my list, but I have different questions for her."

"Tell me what you need. And I'm not sending you any more whiskey, you hear me? If yours can't stand on its own, you can move yourselves home to Ireland and come back to work for the family."

"Dad, I don't need any whiskey. I haven't needed any in more than a year. In fact, I just gave away the last of it last night."

"You gave it away? Maeve..." The warning note in his voice was unpleasantly familiar.

"My private store, Dad. Can we not fight about whiskey today?" He was still none too pleased that his two youngest children not only had no intention of coming back home to work with the family, but were achieving far more success with their own whiskey than any of them had ever dreamed. After her mother had backed Maeve's decision to strike out on her own with a generous gift of her own money, Cathal had reluctantly agreed to support them. But he still wasn't thrilled about it. Maeve was used to the weekly digs about her moving home, but that didn't mean she enjoyed them. Having an ocean between them for these conversations was far preferable to having them in person, though. "I didn't call about the business, actually. I have a different question."

"What have ye gotten yourself into now?"

She sighed and powered through. "I'm volunteering with a nonprofit—" She ignored his audible snort. "And they've just gotten word that a developer intends to buy out their building and force them to stop operating."

"That's a shame." His voice indicated that he didn't really care.

"I want your advice. How can I stop it? You're the one who taught me how to fight back." She still remembered his large hands over hers, gently curving her fingers into tiny fists. *"If they give you hell, Maevey, you give it right back."* She didn't like giving hell. She'd given hugs instead, and he'd despaired of her long ago.

"Maevey, sometimes it's not worth fighting." He sounded tired.

She felt tears sting her eyes. "There's always something worth fighting for, Dad."

"Some old building? Fight for yourself, Maeve. You don't need to go up against some developer. You own your place outright. Focus on the whiskey first; help others second. You can't move forward without a place to stand."

"I have a place to stand, Dad! Whitman's is *fine!*" She felt her voice rising and her stomach twisting. God, she hated arguing. "I just want to know what you would do if you were me."

"I wouldn't be spending all my time petting cats and kissing babies, that's for sure."

"Dad."

"Maevey, I don't have any advice for you. Sometimes this is just the way of the world. Progress waits for no man. Or woman, in your case, I suppose."

"It's not *progress*, Dad; it's condos."

"So buy one. That dinky little house you rent is no place to raise a family."

"A *family*?"

"You're not getting any younger, Maevey. Your mum wants more grandkids."

"You have three other children. And I don't see you nagging Iain." Her brother and Naomi were happily childfree. How they'd managed to get both of their families to stop asking them about it was beyond her. Just imagining the conversation made her break out into a cold sweat, and she *wanted* kids someday. "We're not talking about this. We're talking about how to help an organization that doesn't deserve to get shut down for no reason."

"It's a nonprofit. I doubt they have the firepower to fight back in any meaningful way, no matter how hard you might wish for it." She pictured him shrugging. "Best find a new place to spend your free time."

She gritted her teeth and gave up. "Never mind. I'll find another way. Say hi to the lads for me."

"Call your mam," he said.

The phone went dead and she resisted the urge to throw it across the room.

Well, that had been a supreme waste of effort. Maybe she'd feel better after talking with her mother.

An hour later, refreshed by Colleen Brennan's genuine glee about the article—and the smug knowledge that her father would be annoyed not only by her being on the cover, but also that she hadn't told him about it herself—she realized that her stomach was growling. She'd skipped breakfast in favor of brainstorming, but it hadn't helped at all. Maybe food would help her think.

She headed down to the deli on the corner a block away and ordered her favorite sandwich—half turkey, half roast beef on one slice of rye and one of whole grain, with gouda cheese, tomatoes, pickles, and mustard. It wasn't on the menu, but she ate here at least once a week and they were willing to make it specially for her.

As she paid, she heard a deep voice behind her. "That sounds amazing. Can I have what she's having?"

She turned, and a stranger grinned at her. Sandy brown hair carefully mussed, and an intriguing cleft to his chin. He had on a polo shirt that stretched tight over his chest muscles, and his fitted jeans didn't leave much to the imagination. *Well, hello.* She smiled. "You have good taste."

"So do you." He moved to stand next to her and took out his wallet. "Can I buy you lunch?"

"Oh, I've already paid. Thanks, though." She watched as he handed over a ten dollar bill and accepted his change. He dropped the coins in the tip jar and turned to her.

"I'm Steve."

"Maeve."

"Nice to meet you."

Impulsively, she gestured to a table. "Are you eating here?"

He glanced at his watch. "Actually, I can't. I have a meeting."

"Ah." *Must not be meant to be, then.*

"But…" He searched her face, then smiled. "Could I get your number?" She stared at him, and he must have thought she was about to pepper spray him. He raised his sandwich to his chest as though it might protect him. "Sorry! I'm not creepy, I swear! I'm just new here, and I don't usually meet people who like the same sandwiches I do. And you're really pretty." He bit his lip, like he hadn't meant to say that last part. She didn't miss the fact that his eyes flicked down to her chest before they popped back up and met her gaze.

But she'd done the same thing, hadn't she? His jeans fit very nicely, after all. "Sure." She tore off the blank end of her receipt and snagged a pen from the counter to write her name and phone number down, then handed it to him.

"Thanks," he said, then smiled at her again. "I'll text you."

He dashed out the door, and she picked up her sandwich again and shrugged. Maybe he'd text her, maybe he wouldn't. He seemed nice enough. And she still had lunch either way. Win-win.

HE TEXTED her two hours later.

Unknown Number: Hey, it's Steve from the deli. It was really great to meet you. And that sandwich was delicious.

Maeve: Mine was, too.

She added him in to her contacts as 'Deli Steve.'

Deli Steve: Would you possibly like to get dinner or a drink sometime? I realize we just met and it's a little pushy, but I like to close deals fast.

He added a wink emoji, and she rolled her eyes. It wasn't her favorite pickup line, but he was cute. And there were those cobwebs in her undercarriage to think about.

Maeve: I don't know about deals, but I'd love to get a drink. When are you free?

Deli Steve: Thursday night?

Maeve: Sounds good.

Deli Steve: Where's decent?

Maeve: Frankie's is the best. Meet you there at seven?

Deli Steve: Can't wait.

She put her phone away with a grin. No need to mention all the eyeballs that would be on them there. She didn't want to scare him off. But she *did* want friendly faces around for her first date in ages. Naomi and Angelica thought she needed to get laid? Well, she could find her own sexy stranger, thank you very much.

She gave herself exactly two seconds to think wistfully how nice it would be if Ben was the one asking her out, and then shook her head firmly. *Not going there.* She'd need a friend like Ben if Deli Steve turned out to be a swing and a miss, since it seemed like he wouldn't put her on the spot to find out what had gone wrong they way Angelica and Naomi maybe would.

Now that her personal life was settled, it was time to put her head down and figure out how to save Youth Mentors. She pulled out her notepad again and got to work.

8

———

*B*en was skating on thin ice with his manager. With a local wine festival taking place that weekend, The Hollow Bean was busier than usual and he was struggling to keep up. He'd been warned once already that the next time he fucked up an order, it was coming out of his pay.

Unfortunately, all these tourists kept ordering drinks that sounded more like dessert than coffee. What the hell was a warm and toasty graham cracker latte anyhow? According to Corey, the harried barista toiling away next to him, it was an abomination. And now he had to make three of them for a group of blonde twenty-somethings dressed identically in skinny jeans, tight white t-shirts, and puffy black vests who were waiting impatiently for their orders.

"Hey." A tall guy with a loud, booming voice stepped up to the counter and waved his cup in front of Ben's face. "This isn't what I ordered."

Under the watchful eye of his manager, Ben took the

to-go cup from the man's hands and checked the cardboard sleeve to find out what it was supposed to have been. It turned out the problem wasn't with the drink itself; rather, that the guy had grabbed the wrong order.

"Unless your name is Nancy, I'd think not," Ben replied, taking note of what it was so he could make another one for the *actual* Nancy before she complained too.

"What did you say to me?"

Ben gritted his teeth. He'd only worked at The Hollow Bean for a couple of months, but during that time he'd seen the worst of humanity. So many people treated service staff like complete garbage. He just hoped he hadn't been one of them back in the day. "Just let me get these coffees to them—" he lifted his chin to indicate the three blondes "—and I'll remake yours."

The guy harrumphed, but didn't add anything else. Probably because his gaze was glued to the girls, his eyes raking over the tallest one with undisguised greed. It was a look Ben recognized well—it was the one he wore whenever he was in the same room as Maeve and he thought she wasn't looking.

Having successfully handed over three graham cracker whatevers, he set about remaking the guy's drink, trying not to eavesdrop on the phone conversation he was having.

"I should be able to wrap this up in a week or two," he was saying. "The company that currently occupies the building is a nonprofit so they won't be able to fight Hartwell for long. Mmm-hmm. Yeah, that's right. Kids Matter, Teach Younger, Mentor Forever ... something like that. I know it definitely has to do with kids. Exactly. We should expect some push back from the community because of that, but I figure once Hartwell ponies up a few grand for a new playground or something, that should shut the yokels up. You know how small towns are."

Ben abandoned the milk he'd been foaming and Corey slammed down the bottle of hazelnut syrup he'd just picked up. Ben looked around, noting that the *entire* coffee shop had come to a silent standstill—something Coffee Douche was completely oblivious to.

"Look, that's not my problem. My job is to get in, get the papers signed, and get the fuck out. Why should I care about some kids I'll never meet? You know how these bleeding heart liberals are. They want to help everyone, and meanwhile, they're not actually helping anyone. The condos will do a lot more for this ridiculous town than some old abandoned school, you know?"

With a fury he'd never felt before, Ben untied his apron strings and pulled the fabric over his head, dropping it into the bin of used linens. He had no idea what had come over him, but hearing this guy talk about this mentoring organization so dismissively made him want to do something proactive to stop it.

He felt a hand on his elbow, slowing him down. "What are you doing?" Corey hissed. "You can't knock the fucker out. You'll *definitely* get fired then."

Ben lifted the wooden counter that separated employees from customers and stepped through. Dropping it back down, he turned to Corey. "Oh, I'm going to fight him, all right. Just not how you expect."

They thought this takeover was going to be a walk in the park? Well, the joke was on this Hartwell character because he was going to have to go through him first. River Hill was just a town full of yokels, huh? They didn't think the nonprofit would be able to put up a fight because they couldn't afford a fancy lawyer? He might not work for a high profile firm anymore, but that didn't mean he couldn't go toe to toe with the best of 'em. Hell, a few short months ago he had *been* the best. It was time to brush off the rust and prove he still had what it took to win cases. This asshole and the developers he worked for were going down.

HE STOOD on the sidewalk and stared up at the building he'd decided to save. *No pressure or anything, Worthington.*

With one final deep breath, he made his way slowly up the front steps, wondering the entire time if he was being stupid. You didn't just decide to go back to practicing law because some asshole had been spouting off about how easily he was going to crush the little guy, did you? It was ridiculous that he thought he could help them. And yet, it had been so long since he'd felt so inspired. He knew he'd regret it if he didn't at least try.

Overhead, a bell chimed, and a familiar face looked up from the front desk to greet him.

Immediately, Maeve's expression morphed into a big grin. "Hey you," she said, pushing her chair back to stand. "Did I forget we were meeting for lunch?"

He shook his head in response, unable to form words.

Why didn't Youth Mentors have pictures of their volunteers up on their website or something? Didn't they realize people needed to know who they were going to encounter when they walked through that front door? If he'd known *this* was Maeve's latest volunteering venture, he would have prepared differently.

He swallowed deeply. How did he tell her what he'd heard at the coffee shop? Suddenly, he was assailed with doubt. He'd wanted to do a good thing, but now he felt added pressure knowing that the woman he might be falling for would be personally affected too.

"So," he said, rocking back on his heels.

"What's up?" she asked, her smile dipping into a confused frown. "Is something wrong?"

"No. I mean yes. I mean … shit." He pulled in a deep breath and readied himself to crush her spirits. " This place is in trouble, Maeve."

"I know," she sighed, her eyes shining bright.

In that moment, he nearly rushed forward and pulled her into his arms. Instead, he used that emotion to push away his earlier doubt. He was going to fight this takeover because it was the right thing to do, but he was also going to do it for her.

"I'm going to help, Maeve. I'm going to fight it." He tried to ignore the hopeful look on her face, lest it turn out that he couldn't deliver on his promise. He didn't want to disappoint her.

"You are?" she asked, stepping around the desk and coming to stand in front of him. "How?"

"So, um. You know I used to be a lawyer...back when I was still a d-bag?" His lips quirked to the side, remembering that conversation. So much had changed since then.

"Yeah, I remember."

"Well, um, my area of expertise is real estate law, and despite what the barista gig may indicate, I was good at it. But the thing is, I don't have much experience *saving* buildings so much as acquiring them. And, uh, getting them torn down." He winced.

She crossed her arms over her chest in a protective gesture. "Sort of like the company that's trying to shut us down, then?"

He looked up at her sheepishly. "Exactly like the company that's trying to shut you down."

"So how does that help us?"

"Because I'm not just good at it, Maeve. I'm the best. Better than the guy who's here in River Hill to see this deal go through. Trust me. I've met him, and he's nothing but a pompous windbag. He'll never see me coming."

She stared at him for a long moment, and he watched as so many different emotions flashed through her expressive green eyes, the final one a stab to the heart. It was defeat. "We can't afford a lawyer, Ben. We literally have zero money to fight this."

"I'll do it pro bono."

Her eyes went round. "You'll take the case for free?"

He nodded in the affirmative.

"Oh my god, Ben! You're the best." All at once she launched herself into his arms and hugged him tight.

Ben stiffened, and willed his body not to react. Slowly, he wrapped his arms around her and hugged her too. *Friends hugged*, he told himself as he patted her back the same way he did to his grandma when they hugged. *This isn't sexual. Don't make it into something it's not. And don't you dare poke her with your penis when all she wants is a damned hug.*

He disentangled himself from her embrace. Before she leaned away, Maeve kissed him on the cheek and then bounced on her toes, her body vibrating with energy. "I can't wait for you to tell Joan."

"I can't make any promises, except that I promise to try."

Maeve's smile transformed from one of excitement to fondness. "You really are a good guy, Ben Worthington."

Except maybe he wasn't.

In all the excitement over the takeover, he realized he'd never gotten around to apologizing for having propositioned her the night they'd been at the distillery. That *definitely* wasn't good guy behavior. "That sounds great. But, uh...about the other night. I wanted to thank you."

"The other night?" Her head tilted to the side and she studied him intently.

"Yeah, it was a dick move to say what I said. I'm really sorry, and I wanted to thank you for, um, sending me home. You know? Honestly, aside from Max, I don't have a lot of people I'm close to. I'd hate it if I did something to jeopardize our friendship. It's too valuable to me."

"Right," she said, rubbing the toe of her shoe back and forth over the cracked linoleum. "Our friendship. Of course. Don't worry about it. Honestly, I'd forgotten all about it."

"You had?"

She waved her hand in front of her face. "Totally water under the bridge, as you Americans say. Who hasn't gotten drunk and said something inappropriate? I used to do it all the time." She laughed easily and turned toward her desk. "Let's get you in to see Joan, shall we?"

Ben stood rooted to the floor, a strange sort of disappointment washing over him. He'd meant what he said: he valued her friendship and he never wanted to do anything to compromise it. Still, for one brief moment he'd let himself imagine a different response...one where she told him that she'd *wanted* him to make a move on her. One where she laughed and said that she would have climbed him like a tree if he hadn't been falling down drunk. One where she confessed that she thought about him every waking moment too.

Only, she hadn't. So now he needed to do what Maeve had said and put it behind them. Water under the bridge, indeed.

"All right." He put one foot in front of the other and followed her out of the foyer and down a long, drab hall. "Let's go talk to Joan and figure out how we save this place." He might not get the girl, Ben reasoned, but something good could come from this. At least he hoped so.

9

Ben had *thanked* her for not sleeping with him. Maeve had thought the night they'd escaped Angelica and Naomi's matchmaking had been embarrassing, but this went so far beyond that. It was like the difference between stubbing your toe and breaking every bone in your body. And to think she'd been on the verge of blurting out that she'd nearly called him that morning to tell him to come over and finish what he'd started.

But when he'd made it clear that he was *grateful* she hadn't taken him up on his drunken offer, she'd nearly died. He wanted to stay friends? Fine, there were worse things in the world. Especially considering they *did* have a good thing going.

Besides, she didn't need him. She had a date! A real one, too! And if the the looks Deli Steve had tossed her way during their brief exchange were anything to go by, he wasn't the type of guy who'd rescind an offer of sex. Or apologize for it. Thank goodness she was meeting up with him sooner rather than later. She needed an ego boost, and he could be the perfect man to give it to her. She just hoped things didn't go sideways there, too. She couldn't take any more humiliation this week.

Maeve sat back down at the front desk with an audible thump. Utterly uninspired, she rifled through the papers she'd been sorting and filing when Ben had first walked in. She should feel better, shouldn't she? He seemed confident that he could do all the lawyerly things that needed to be done to stop the developers from taking over the building. But he'd also said he knew things from the other side of the equation, something that made her belly do a sick little flop when she thought about it. She imagined Ben in a sharp suit, arguing in a courtroom, and her mind threw that up against the memory of Joan weeping behind her desk. She didn't want to believe that Ben had been just like the people who were trying to close down this place. She just had to hope that he was better than they were.

She also needed to re-evaluate her priorities. What kind of woman was ready to rip off one man's clothes while getting ready to go on a date with another? Poor Steve. They hadn't even gone out yet and already she felt as if she was emotionally cheating on him. She really had to stop thinking about Ben.

The door to the back office opened, and he and Joan came out. The older woman was smiling broadly, and Ben looked cheerful, too. "So you'll gather the info and email it over to me?" he asked.

"I'm going to get started on it right now," Joan

answered. "Maeve, can I use that computer? Most of our files are there."

"Sure." She rose to let Joan sit. "After this is over, let's talk about backing up your data, though." She heard Ben chuckle. "Do you need anything else from me?"

"Mm, not right now." Joan's tone was absent-minded as she focused intensely on the computer and clicked her way through the file structure. "It's probably faster for me to just gather everything, since I know where it is. Why don't you go to lunch?"

"Who can say no to lunch?" Maeve grinned at her boss, but the other woman wasn't even looking at her.

"I'll walk you out," Ben said.

"Want to get lunch?" She waited until they were outside to ask. She didn't need Joan to witness their new hotshot lawyer shooting her down.

But he surprised her by agreeing. "Sure. If I'm going to be researching property records I definitely need to do it on a full stomach."

"What sort of food goes best with property records?" she asked.

"Baked goods," he replied with an absolutely straight face.

She laughed. "The Breadery it is, then."

The building that Youth Mentors occupied was only a few blocks away from River Hill's picturesque town square, so they walked to lunch, chatting about the work Maeve was doing and the building they were trying to save.

"There are birds nesting in the eaves," Maeve said. "It's cute."

He looked thoughtful. "Do you know what kind of birds?"

She shook her head. "I've never been much for birdwatching. I have an uncle who likes it, though. Why?"

"There was a case a few years ago that was referred to the Environmental Protection Agency because a rare bird was nesting in a tree in front of a building that was set to be torn down. They wound up leaving everything untouched to protect its nesting area."

"Hmm." She thought about it, trying to remember what the birds looked like and coming up blank. "I'm not sure, to be honest. What if they turn out to be common sparrows?"

He grinned at her as he opened the door to The Breadery. "Oh, that's just *one* weapon in our arsenal. I'm just getting started."

Something had changed in Ben; something that made him a little more focused and intense. Maybe him using his skills for good was what he'd needed to move past the burnout he'd described. Unfortunately for her, this extra confidence made him even more appealing. She needed to ignore the way his grin made her want to kiss him.

"What do you want to get?" she asked, pushing that thought deep into the recesses of her brain where it would hopefully stay hidden.

He looked at the glass case. "Do they have apple fritters today? I heard they were good."

"Not today." Sean appeared behind the case. "Hi, guys. What can I get you?"

"Ben needs research sustenance," Maeve informed him. "Lots of carbs."

Sean grinned. "Carbs are our specialty. Take your pick."

"Those scones look good." Ben pointed to the second row of baked goods..

"They are. I use a Mexican spice blend straight from my in-laws." Sean pulled out the tray. "How many can I get you?"

"I want one," Maeve said. She'd had a few of the recipes Jess and Sean cooked up together and she wasn't about to turn this one down.

"In that case, I'll take two," Ben said.

"My treat," Maeve blurted. She hated that his finances were something he was sensitive about, but she couldn't let him pay for stuff when she could easily afford it. "You're working pro bono, remember?"

"Pro bono? You lawyering again?" Sean asked as he pulled out three scones and dropped them into a parchment-lined bag.

"He's going to save Youth Mentors," Maeve told the baker, ignoring Ben's wince.

"Don't jinx me," he said.

She looked up at him in alarm. "Is that a thing?"

He laughed. "No, we'll win." His easy statement rolled over her like a wave of warmth. "But I haven't even started my research yet. Let's not show our hand all over town. No offense, Sean," he added quickly.

"None taken. I won't spill your secret to any other lawyers who come in here to buy scones," Sean said dryly.

They took their orders to go and headed out to the

town square, angling their walk toward where they'd started. "Are you heading back to help out?" Ben asked.

Maeve shrugged. "If Joan needs me. If not, I'll drive over to the distillery and work on a few things there. You?"

"I should probably go back to the Bean. I kind of ran out of there."

She blinked. "You what?"

"Yeah, I heard the lawyer who served Joan with the papers talking on his phone and he pissed me off so much I ran straight over to help."

She laughed. "Not the noblest motivation, but I'll take it. I'm glad you did."

"Me too." They were both silent for a moment. "What do you have going on this week?"

She thought over her schedule. "Meeting a distributor tomorrow, and then running a tasting the day after. Oh! I have a date on Thursday." She looked up with a smile, waiting to share her excitement with him.

"A date?" He swallowed, and she realized she couldn't identify the expression on his usually mobile face.

She nodded and pushed her hair behind her ears. She didn't know why she suddenly felt nervous talking to him about this, only that she did. But they were friends, and friends could talk about their dates, right?

"A guy at the deli asked me out. We're going to meet at Frankie's for drinks. I figure that way I've got built-in eyes on me in case he turns out to be a creep. And if he's not, somebody can report back to Angelica and Naomi that they can lay off me."

"You mean, if they don't come barreling through the

door to see for themselves within five minutes of you arriving." He started walking again, and she skipped a couple of steps to catch up to his longer strides.

"Exactly."

"So. Sex with a stranger?"

"A stranger of my choosing." She mock shuddered and tucked her arm into his. "That was an awful night, although I'm glad we got to be friends because of it."

"Our Mutual Embarrassment Society really panned out, huh?" His voice was still oddly rough.

"Sure did. What about you?"

"What about me?"

"Got any dates lined up?" She was morbidly curious. He was clearly interested in sex, but drunk propositions aside, not with her. Friendship without benefits. Surely, then, he must be looking elsewhere.

"No. Nothing." He answered her quickly, and his pace increased to the point where she was nearly running to keep up.

She grabbed his arm. "Whoa. Slow down."

"Sorry." He stopped completely. They were near her car. "Are you going inside or just heading out?"

She thought about it. Joan didn't need her help to gather information, and she'd finished pretty much everything else. "I'm going over to the distillery."

He nodded. "I'll leave you here, then. Gotta go save my job and then get some research done."

"What are you going to tell them?"

He shrugged. "The truth. The entire place went dead when that asshole started running his mouth."

"Ben..." She swallowed. "You can't really afford to take

any time off, can you?" She knew he didn't like to talk about his money. Or rather, his lack thereof.

He frowned. "I'll make it work." She opened her mouth, but he interrupted her with a sudden grin. "Maybe when I win this case, I'll get a new lawyer job. Back in business, baby." He nudged her elbow.

She was too frozen to respond. Ben wanted to work as a lawyer again? Taking on this one case to save Youth Mentors was one thing, but his old job had been the exact opposite. How could he want to go back? He'd said it himself; he'd been miserable. More than that, he'd been fired. Not that she thought he wanted to be a barista forever, but...she realized she had no idea what Ben's future plans were.

Her heart plummeted. Maybe the man she'd gotten to know these past couple of months wasn't the real Ben. What if her new friend was actually the midlife crisis version of him? Suddenly she felt like crying.

10

*B*en pulled open the dirty glass door and stepped into the sparsely furnished office located in a strip mall on the industrial edge of town. It took his eyes a moment to adjust, and when they did he was gratified to see that even though the developer's lawyer talked a big game, he worked in a shit hole. The room was practically empty, save for a large, dented metal desk, a fake, dusty plant, and a water dispenser that glugged every couple of seconds. It was the sort of place corporations begrudgingly rented for temporary minions who didn't deserve better.

A door on the far end opened, and the other lawyer— who Ben recognized from a photo captioned 'S. Smith' on the Hartwell Properties website—stopped short. "Can I help you?" He tossed a rolled up magazine onto a folding chair just outside the door.

Charming.

Ben sauntered— strutted, actually—over to the man's

desk and dropped a manila folder filled with copies of the motions, counter-motions, and injunctions he'd spent the last two days filing on behalf of Youth Mentors. The bundle also included a notice from the EPA saying they were going to investigate the site to determine whether or not the nest Maeve had seen belonged to an American peregrine falcon. If so, these guys could kiss their River Hill condos goodbye. They might eventually be able to work through all the bureaucratic red tape Ben intended to create for them with the other motions he'd filed—things like historic property registration, property line contestation, and even a questionable lien on the city's ownership of the property—but it would take months and no developer wanted to take on on that type of overhead. Even if they got through all of that, as a rule, developers did *not* want to tangle with animal rights activists. He knew this from first-hand experience.

"What's that?" Smith asked, tilting his chin toward the envelope. "You're not serving me with papers again, are you? If that bitch ex-girlfriend of mine wants child support—"

"Those, you asshole, are all the reasons why your boss should pull up stakes and build elsewhere."

"Yeah, that's not going to happen."

"You sure about that?" Ben slid his hands into his pockets casually and rocked back on his heels. He'd dealt with guys like this before. He knew it was only a matter of time until the other man lost his shit. All he had to do was exercise a bit of patience. Thankfully, Ben had all the time in the world.

Smith pushed the sleeves of his shirt up his forearms and advanced on Ben with a scowl. "You sure you want to come into my place of business and put on this tough guy act with me? You don't know who you're fucking with."

Actually, Ben *did* know, and he wasn't the least bit frightened. He'd had no trouble at all finding out more about Hartwell's S. Smith from a quick search of court records. As it turned out, this guy was notorious for making threats that he never actually backed up with action. He was a straight up bully who talked a big game and got people to back down through lies and intimidation. What he didn't know, of course, was that Ben had already hit rock bottom. There was nothing this man could threaten him with that hadn't already happened. For the first time since he'd been escorted out of that SoMa high rise, he felt free.

"You're going to come into my office and insult me? Do you know who I am?" Smith was still ranting.

Ben stood his ground. "I know *exactly* who you are, and here's a word of advice: the next time you roll into town intent on disrupting the fabric of the community, maybe keep your opinions about the yokels to yourself. Oh, and don't steal other people's coffee, *Nancy*."

"Who the fuck is Nancy? Better yet, who the fuck are you?" He grabbed the envelope and ripped it open. After reviewing the top couple of pages, his angry gaze popped back up to meet Ben's calm one. "What the hell is this? The goddamn EPA? Those hippies managed to find a lawyer stupid enough to take on their case?"

"No. They found one who was good enough to *win* their case."

The other man glared at Ben for a few beats, his expression going from angry, to confused, and then finally recognition. "Wait a minute. You're the coffee guy; you're no lawyer."

"I am a lawyer. I work at a coffee shop. Two separate things." Ben turned on his heels and strolled toward the door, then paused. "Oh, before I forget. Make sure your client signs page ten. I wouldn't want to have to sue them for negligence, too." He pushed open the door and stepped out into the sunshine, leaving Smith sputtering behind him.

Ben chuckled as he climbed into his BMW, relishing the befuddled look on the other man's face. Ever since he'd decided to help out Youth Mentors, he had been looking forward to using that line. *Ed*, an old show about a lawyer who'd lost his job in New York City and had moved home to Ohio to run a law firm out of a bowling alley, had been one of his favorites back in the day. In fact, it was the title character who'd made him want to become a lawyer in the first place.

God, he'd missed this.

Most people thought being a lawyer was boring. And it could be—all those hours of researching past cases for precedence, or searching the books for some obscure loophole they could use to get a case thrown out. But it could be exhilarating, too. In fact, Ben thought those long hours spent poring over legal tomes were all part of the thrill of the chase.

Just when you thought you'd hit a dead end, you'd dump another cup of coffee down your throat and dive back in, determined to find the thing that could be the difference between winning and losing your case. And then, bleary eyed and lacking sleep, you would, and all those hours hunched over a desk, your finger turning yellow from the highlighter you'd been gripping for hours on end, would be worth it. You'd saved the day. You'd walk into the office the next day, showered and freshly shaved, your thousand dollar suit molded to your body, and the team would clap and tell you what a badass you were.

Except now there was no office to go back to. He didn't have a team of interns and junior associates who'd fawn all over him and tell him they couldn't wait to be like him someday. There was no Michelin-starred restaurant the partners would take him to and pass him a hefty bonus. There was only his tiny studio apartment over Max's garage, and Frankie's, the nicest restaurant in a twenty mile radius, would have to do for his round of celebratory drinks.

And he definitely had something to celebrate. A horn blared behind him, and Ben snapped back to attention. He flipped on his blinker and turned toward home, his car shooting forward with purpose. For the first time in months, he knew what he wanted.

BEN PRACTICALLY RAN up the stairs to his apartment, yanking his tie loose as he went. The suits—as good as they looked, and as much as they appealed to the opposite sex—were something he'd never learned to enjoy about being a lawyer. He was a t-shirts and jeans kind of guy. Always had been, always would be. As he pulled a soft, time-worn shirt he'd owned for over a decade on over his head, he took one final look at himself in the mirror and mussed his hair just so.

It was longer than it had ever been, but he kind of liked it. Briefly, he wondered if he'd have to get a haircut now that he'd decided to go back to work. Part of him hoped not. Whenever he imagined Maeve kissing him (which usually happened when he was standing naked in the shower), she was frequently fisting a hunk of his hair in her hands and tugging on it. Strange as it was, the fantasy of her pulling his hair was something he didn't want to do away with by cutting it all off.

Fifteen minutes later, he opened the door to Frankie's and scanned the crowd, his gaze landing on Max behind the bar mixing drinks while he chatted with Noah and Sean. With a spring in his step, he sailed through the crowd and pulled up a stool next to them. "Gentlemen."

Max did a double take, and his eyes bounced between the other two men. "Hey. I thought you were busy tonight."

He'd told his friends what he was doing, and they'd had a few notes about the historical relevance of the building that had been helpful. Sean had grown up in River Hill, and Noah and Max had lived here for a long time, so they'd been able to provide him with a few small details that Ben would have otherwise spent hours searching for. Not that he wouldn't have found them, but he appreciated the help. More than appreciated it.

He reached for a printed menu. "I wrapped things up early. Turns out I still got it."

"That sounds like a good thing." There was a slight note of hesitation in Noah's voice that Ben didn't understand, and therefore chose to ignore.

"It's a *very* good thing." He finally felt like he had his mojo back. He finally felt like himself.

For months, he'd floated through life with nothing to ground him. The only thing he knew how to do was something he'd no longer wanted to. These guys, as awesome as they were, couldn't understand that. With their James Beard awards and *Wine Spectator* accolades they were on top of their game—and they lived for it.

He paused and reconsidered that line of thinking. Sean could probably sympathize. After all, he'd been a hot shot record executive down in L.A. representing some of the biggest names in pop music before his life had imploded and he'd moved home to figure his shit out. Although unlike Ben and The Hollow Bean, The Breadery—and the former beauty queen he had met running past it each morning—had been exactly what Sean had needed to gain closure on that dark chapter of his life.

As far as Ben was concerned, once he wrapped things up here, if he never stepped foot in another hipster coffee shop for the rest of his life, it would be too soon.

"You should have seen the guy's face," he continued gleefully. "He didn't know what hit him."

"The EPA thing come through?" Noah asked.

"Sort of. They're sending someone out next week to look at the nest, but the full investigation could take months, and it'll be enough to give the developer second thoughts. No one wants to deal with animal rights activists. Those fuckers have nothing but time on their hands, and righteous indignation to fuel them."

"Don't be a dick." Max shot him an exasperated glare.

Ben winced. "Sorry, that came out wrong. I'm not some uncaring asshole. I love nature, honestly. But developers *hate* dealing with that shit because it can tie a project up for years. And it turns out I love seeing those guys stymied. Besides, it's for the children." He smirked, and Max rolled his eyes as he poured Ben a drink.

He didn't bother asking Ben what he wanted. They'd been born and raised in Portland—the answer was always craft beer. The more local, the better, and Max had a great one on draught.

"More like you're doing it for Maeve," Max muttered loudly, causing Noah to cough on the taco he'd been inhaling.

"I don't know what you're talking about." Ben tried to paste an innocent look on his face.

"Sure you don't," Max said, passing him the beer.

"When did you guys get together?" Sean asked just before popping a chip into his mouth.

Ben stared down into his beer while he considered his answer. The epiphany about his career wasn't the only one he'd had that afternoon. He'd also decided he was going to tell Maeve how he felt. She was the first person he thought of when he woke up in the morning, and the last face he pictured before he went to bed at night.

Unfortunately, he still didn't know if they had a future together. And until he was sure he could be the man she needed, he didn't want to start something he couldn't finish. Max had been right: Maeve was a forever kind of girl, not someone you fucked around with while you figured your shit out.

"We're not together," he eventually said, catching Max's eyes over the rim of his glass while taking a deep pull of his IPA. With that one look, he communicated a wealth of information to his lifelong best friend. *Not yet. I hope.*

Noah clapped him on the shoulder, a little too hard. "That's probably good, since she just walked in with another guy."

Ben turned on his stool and his heart plummeted to somewhere around his knees. Her head was thrown back and she was laughing, her arm looped through her date's. In his excitement over the afternoon's developments, he'd completely forgotten that she'd told him she had a date tonight with some guy she'd met at the deli.

Sure you did, his subconscious chided. *You knew she'd be here, and that's exactly why you showed up too. You wanted to get a look at the competition.*

Begrudgingly, Ben realized that was true. Which said a lot more about his frame of mind than he liked. He couldn't fault Maeve for agreeing to go out with somebody else. It wasn't like he'd actually gotten up the balls to ask her himself. He'd been giving her all kinds of mixed signals, talking about friendship and then staring at her mouth for far too long. This was his own damn fault. So here she was, on a date with some other guy. He'd just have to hope that it didn't go well. Which was remarkably uncharitable of him. He winced internally.

It was only when he took a second look at the pair that Ben realized just *who* her date was. And *that* was when he saw red. He was off his stool and shouldering his way through the crowd toward them before he realized what he was doing.

11

"What the hell is this?" Ben's angry voice startled Maeve out of her laughter, although she was really only being polite. The joke hadn't been that good to begin with.

"Ben?" She stared at him uncertainly. Why did he look so mad? Movement caught her eye, and she saw Angelica standing behind Ben, her eyes wide as she held onto Noah's arm, murmuring something to him. She felt Steve stiffen next to her, but then he suddenly relaxed and threw his arm around her, tugging her in close to his side. She looked up just in time to see him smiling at Ben. It wasn't a particularly pleasant smile. It looked … predatory.

Great. She hadn't come here to be fought over. She'd come here for a drink. "Come on, Steve," she said. She tugged him toward the bar, ignoring Ben stalking after them like some kind of giant predator. His hair *was* kind of lion-esque. But she didn't need to be thinking about how he'd look right before he sprang at her.

She slid onto a stool at the bar, meeting Max's eyes. "A beer, please." For some reason she wasn't in the mood for cocktails, even with her own whiskey.

Max pulled her a pint of her favorite without saying anything. He slid it across the counter with his eyes mostly on Ben, communicating something she didn't understand. Exasperated, she turned to the looming presence behind her while Steve ordered his own drink.

"*What*?"

"You can't possibly be here with him," Ben announced flatly.

"She is, buddy, so let it go. Take the *loss*." Steve emphasized the word oddly, and Maeve glanced at him, feeling her eyebrows draw down.

"Do you know who this guy is?" Ben stayed focused on Maeve, ignoring her date. Being the center of his undivided attention was making her tingle in places friends usually didn't, damn it. That searing focus she'd seen when he was explaining his plan to save Youth Mentors was suddenly applied directly to her, and it felt like she was stepping directly into the sun.

"What does it matter?" He was the one who wanted to be friends. He'd thanked her for not having sex with him. She drew that memory around her like a cloak as she glared at him. "We met at the deli. I told you about it."

"Do you know what he does for a living?"

Her patience snapped. "Not *yet*. If you'd let me have my date, maybe I could find out."

His lips thinned in what appeared to be fury. "He's a lawyer, Maeve."

"So are you." Had Steve just snorted? What was going on here?

Ben raised his arm as though he might hit the other man. Suddenly Noah was there, his big form dwarfing all of them, as he gently put a hand on Ben's shoulder. The pressure kept Ben's arm from going any further. He settled for pointing at Steve, his finger jabbing as far forward as Noah would let it. "He's the lawyer who served Youth Mentors with paperwork. He's the one trying to shut you down."

Maeve's entire field of vision went blank. "He's what?" She turned and stared at Steve, who was looking back at her with a bored expression.

"I work for a developer, yeah. You do something with that kids group? Too bad, I guess." He shrugged. "Maybe you can find some other way to spend your time." His grin gave every indication that he had some ideas he wouldn't mind exploring with her.

Her beer glass was in her hand before she had a conscious thought, and she'd upturned it over his head before she'd even processed that she was holding it.

He came to his feet sputtering and swearing. "You bitch!"

Ben did hit him, then.

"Oops," Noah said mildly. "Lost my grip."

Steve clung to the bar top, the red mark on his cheek glowing as he shook his head. "You're going to regret this," he told Ben viciously. "None of that crap you filed is going to come through. And your shitty town doesn't even deserve the revenue from the condos Hartwell wants to build."

"Joan Mayfield has done more for this 'shitty town' than you could ever dream." Angelica's voice was hard. "And we don't need the kind of revenue people like you would bring." The actress was an active member of River Hill's tourism board. For all that she'd only lived here a few years, she seemed to know everyone and everything.

"I think you'll find that no matter what happens with the property, you're done here," Ben said. His voice was flatter than Maeve had ever heard it, but it softened when he turned to her. "Maeve?" He was asking all sorts of things, she suspected, but she was too confused and horrified to focus on anything but the immediate.

"Please, get him out of here," she whispered. She'd poured a beer on somebody's head. And she hadn't been the least bit nauseous or nervous about it. Maybe she could handle conflict after all. Just a little.

Max came out from behind the counter and took Steve by the arm. The other man was still yelling at Ben, something about the EPA and birds. Now she was starting to understand why he'd seemed so annoyed when he met up with her earlier. She suspected his day really hadn't gone well. *Thanks to Ben.*

"Come on," Max said. "You're not welcome here."

"You better call your manager about the behavior of your guests," Steve snarled at him.

Max quirked an eyebrow and visibly tightened his grip on the other man's elbow, making him wince. "I'm the owner, actually. And I didn't see anything but you insulting my friends and making an ass out of yourself."

"Like hell you are. No s—" Steve stopped abruptly, showing some sense for possibly the first time in his entire life, Maeve suspected. "Whatever." He tried to shrug off Max's hand and failed. "We'll see who's laughing in court. Your stupid restaurant serves crappy beer anyway. It'll probably go out of business before the condos are even finished."

Somebody cleared their throat, and Maeve turned to see Naomi standing directly underneath the plaque that held Max's James Beard award certificate, tapping it with her fingernail. "Seems unlikely," she drawled. "Can somebody get this moron out of here? I just got here and I'd really like some fresher air."

Max muscled a mostly-silent Steve over to the door while everybody watched. When it slammed behind him, applause erupted from several corners of the restaurant. Max rolled his eyes and waved it off, heading back behind the bar and into the kitchen to check on the food that was being assembled on the large open counters that were visible to diners.

Then it felt like all eyes were on Maeve. She shriveled into herself as she felt the weight of her friends' stares.

"You went on a date with the lawyer who was trying to close down Youth Mentors?" Angelica finally asked.

"I didn't know that's who he was," she protested.

"You didn't take five seconds to verify that he wasn't a murderer? You didn't Google him?" Naomi demanded.

"Pot, kettle," Iain murmured from behind her. Maeve hadn't seen her brother come in after Naomi, so focused had she been on her own misery.

"Our situation was different," Naomi countered. "At least I knew what you did for a living, and vice versa."

"You're the one who told her to have sex with a stranger," Noah pointed out.

"I didn't mean some random jackass lawyer! I meant him!" Naomi pointed at Ben, whose ears turned red.

But not nearly as red as Maeve suspected her own face was. She opened her mouth, but Max had returned just in time to interrupt her. He cocked his thumb toward Ben and said, "To be fair, he's also a random jackass lawyer." The chef seemed to think the entire situation was hilarious, now that Steve was gone.

"Thanks a lot," Ben said.

"Even if you didn't know who he was, what I don't understand is how you could agree to go out with a guy like that." Sean scowled. "Grade-A dickwad."

"He wasn't exactly hiding his stripes," Angelica agreed.

"He didn't seem that bad at the deli." Although now that she thought about it, he'd spent a lot of time looking at her boobs. And that whole liking the same sandwich thing seemed like a line. Nobody liked the same sandwiches she did. Not even Ben.

She glanced over at him, but he was scowling at the floor. Apparently he thought she was a colossal idiot, too. Her heart sank.

"I just wanted to go on a date," she said quietly before turning to Angelica. "I thought I was taking your advice."

Angelica sighed. "Just...be more careful next time, okay?"

Maeve hated it when her friends treated her like a child. They might be older than she was by a few years, but it wasn't as though she wasn't an adult. And Jess was the exact same age she was, yet everyone seemed to think *she* had it all together. Where was Jess, anyway?

The door burst open, and her best friend flew in, breathing hard. "I had to run here! No parking close by. Did I miss it? Are they—oh." She caught sight of Maeve, surrounded by annoyed friends, drooping on a barstool. "Oh, honey, what happened?"

Even Jess pitied her now. Maeve was too overwhelmed by anger and humiliation to speak, but it didn't matter. Sean was already giving Jess a brief overview of the situation.

"The same lawyer? Ouch." Jess winced.

"Yes, let's all keep talking about how stupid I was," Maeve burst out. "Preferably without including me in the conversation. It's great. Super great."

There was dead silence. Finally, Max broke it. "Nobody thinks you're stupid, Maeve."

"Well, I do. You guys are right. I should never have gone out with him. I should have been able to tell what a jerk he was right away. I'm the idiot who went on a date with the person trying to shut down her own organization. Yay, Maeve." She dropped her head onto her forearms on the bar and sighed as she listened to her friends whisper to one another.

They clearly had no idea what to do. Neither did she, honestly. She'd thought she'd reached her limit on humiliation, but apparently the universe and her own terrible taste in dates had other ideas. God. She'd willingly showed up to Frankie's with the sort of man who thought organizations like Youth Mentors didn't matter...thought a place like River Hill would actually benefit from some stupid trendy condos. And literally every single person she knew and loved, not to mention —she raised her head and looked around at the full tables and booths—practically half the town, had been here to witness Steve calling her a bitch. In that moment, it seemed like everyone was staring at her, pitying her, judging her.

She felt tears pricking the back of her eyes as she tried to take deep breaths. A hand landed on her shoulder, and the warmth sliding through her clued her in to whose it was. She raised her head and saw Ben angling his body to block other people's view of her. "You okay?" he murmured.

"Not really."

"I didn't think so. Want to leave?"

She nodded, not trusting herself to speak.

"Okay. Come on, I'll take you home." Somehow, he managed to get her up and moving and past their friends with only the briefest of goodbyes.

12

*B*en and Maeve sat in his car outside of her small ranch-style home on the edge of town, neither of them saying a word. Next to him, she wrung her hands.

"Hey," he said, reaching across the dark cabin to lay a comforting hand on her shoulder. "You didn't know."

She turned her face to him and huffed. "Story of my life."

"No," he said, his hand slipping forward to rest against the exposed skin at the base of her neck. He'd seen her hair tossed into carefree ponytails countless times, but for her date, she'd worn it up an elaborate mix of twisted coils and braids. Small tendrils were escaping from their confinement, and he resisted the urge to twine them around his fingers. Instead, he let his thumb brush back and forth over her nape. "The story of your life is that you're the kindest, most trusting person I've ever known."

Maeve's eyes filled with unshed tears. "Which

translates to being the most naive person you've ever known. Just once, I wish … " She sighed and turned her head to stare out the window. "Never mind. It doesn't matter."

She sounded so bleak, so utterly lost. It was a feeling he knew all too well. He'd been there himself a time or two over the last year. And as cliche as it may have sounded, talking about it had helped. He wanted to be the shoulder she leaned on now the way Max had been his.

"What do you wish?" he asked, his tone gentle, yet probing.

Her shoulders slumped forward. "Let's pretend I never said that."

Ben stared at her for a beat, but when she didn't continue, he reluctantly drew away and busied his hands with knobs on the dash. If he didn't keep them occupied, he was liable to reach out and draw her into his arms instead. She was hurting, and he wanted to comfort her. Yeah, comfort. That's all this overwhelming desire to hold her close and never let go was.

It had absolutely nothing to do with seeing her with another man earlier. Nope, not a thing. His lips twisted as he recognized denial. Ben wasn't a jealous man, but watching Maeve laugh with Steve Smith had pulled at some primal urge he'd never felt before, triggering some deep-seated need to claim her. To call her his own. To protect her.

But Maeve didn't need his protection. She was strong and capable, regardless what their mutual friends seemed to think. So what if she'd made a mistake by trusting someone she shouldn't have? While he'd never really trusted anyone outside of Max (and now Maeve, he conceded), her ability to open herself up to possibility was one of the things he lo—.

No. He shook his head. He didn't *love* her. He couldn't. You didn't fall in love with a woman you'd never even kissed.

Shit. He gripped the steering wheel tight. He was losing his fucking mind over her. The air in the car felt suddenly stifling, and he couldn't seem to pull enough of it into his lungs to breathe properly. He needed to leave.

Ben leaned forward to look out the windshield. In the last couple of minutes, fat droplets of rain had begun to fall, and fog from the river had rolled in. In the distance, the light from her front porch glowed, but otherwise, the landscape was a muted, milky gray.

"I'll walk you in."

She turned back to him and nodded. "Yeah, okay."

"Wait there," he said, opening his door and running around the front of the car to the passenger side. He tugged his jacket off and made a sort of makeshift shelter of it. Maeve stepped out and looked up at him. Damn, she really was the most beautiful woman he'd ever laid eyes on. "This should keep you dry," he said, swallowing past the unwelcome lump that had formed his throat.

"Thank you," she whispered, stepping up onto the curb.

Together, they dashed up her front walk to her door. He held the jacket aloft while she rooted around in her purse for her keys. When she found them, she tossed him a look he had trouble interpreting, and then she moved to unlock the door. She missed the lock, though, and her keychain tumbled to the floor. Simultaneously, they bent to retrieve them, and their hands touched. Ben moved to pull away, but Maeve's fingers twisted around his. With her free hand, she scooped up her keys, and when she looked up at him, she licked her lips.

Ben's heart kicked wildly in his chest as rain pelted down on them, the makeshift umbrella all but forgotten. He forgot everything, in fact, except for how badly he wanted her. And if the heat in her eyes was any indication, she wanted him, too.

"Maeve?"

Her eyes flicked between his for a few brief seconds, and he watched as she drew a breath deep into her lungs, stretching the thin cotton of her dress tight across her chest. "That thing I wished for before?" Her voice was a breathy sigh, and it made him think of all the ways he wanted to make her sigh in the future.

"Yeah?" he asked, his own voice coming out as a rough rasp.

She pushed to her feet, bringing him with her. Ben tried not to fixate on the fact that she hadn't let go of his hand. In fact, she was holding it even tighter, her fingers now laced with his. "How familiar are you with Demi Lovato?"

Ben's brows scrunched in confusion over what seemed like an abrupt change in topic. "I'm sorry, I don't follow."

Maeve stepped close and lifted her face to his. "She has this song called 'Ruin the Friendship.' It's about someone she can't stop thinking about but has stayed away from because he's her good friend—maybe even her best friend. But she's willing to risk the friendship for the sake of one night in his arms."

Ben swallowed deeply. "Are you saying that's what you want? To risk our friendship for what—one night together? And then what? We just pretend it never happened?" Frankly, he didn't know if he was capable of that. He was pretty damn certain that once he got a taste of her, he'd want another, and another, and another. He already ached with desire every damn time he was around her. How bad would his cravings be if he was given a sample of heaven only to have it snatched away?

Maeve chewed on her lip, and her gaze flicked away ... almost as if now that she'd given voice to her desire, she'd lost her nerve to take it any further.

Honestly, he could understand. How many times had he wanted to tell her how he felt, only to chicken out at the last second? How many times had he wanted to reach out and touch her the way he frequently did in his dreams? Too many times to count ... all because he was afraid of ruining their friendship. He might not know a damn thing about Demi Lovato, but he knew the emotions that would drive someone to write a song like that. He knew because he lived with them daily.

Her eyes found his again. "Come inside, Ben."

He wanted to. God, how he wanted. But he hadn't kept his feelings to himself all these weeks to lose her now. He'd rather have Maeve in his life forever as a friend than to spend one night in her bed only for everything to implode the next day.

"I can't, Maeve."

Her eyes fell, and her shoulders slumped in on themselves. She took a step back and then turned toward the door, his fingers sliding from hers as she moved to unlock her door. "I'm sorry. I shouldn't have—"

"I want to," he rushed to say, stepping up behind her and putting his hands on her shoulders. He couldn't *not* touch her. Not after what she'd just offered. "You have no idea how badly."

She glanced at him over her shoulder, and the look in her eyes nearly undid him. Pain. Embarrassment. Doubt. "Then why?"

Ben pulled a deep breath into his lungs and pressed his front to her back, close enough that she could feel the full extent of his desire. His palms coasted down her arms and then back up, leaving goosebumps in their wake. His head fell forward so that his mouth hovered near her ear. "I don't want to lose you."

"You won't," she whispered. "We won't let that happen."

"Do you promise?" His blood spiked with anticipation. He'd tried to do the right thing, but if Maeve was committed to keeping their friendship intact, he could be, too.

At the furthest recesses of his brain, Ben recognized that he was rationalizing his next move. He had no idea what would happen tomorrow, but the truth was, he'd convince himself of anything if it meant he got to have her. Even if it was just for now.

She nodded, her hand twisting the doorknob. "I promise."

He dropped a feather-light kiss on the nape of her

neck, and she shivered in his arms. "Then open the door, Maeve."

———

THE SECOND they stepped over her threshold, Ben scooped Maeve into his arms. She squeaked in surprise, but then her arms went around his neck as his mouth came down to meet hers. No hesitancy, no delay. He'd waited weeks for this moment, and now that it was here, he wasn't going to waste any more time.

"Bedroom?" he asked against her lips.

She untangled her arms and pointed somewhere to the left. Ben raised his eyes long enough to see a narrow hallway, and made his way for it.

"Second door on the left," she said, pressing her mouth to his neck when he paused to figure out which door was hers.

In seconds, he had her splayed out on her bed, her wet clothes clinging to her curves. He stood over her, marveling at how beautiful she looked. How did he get so goddamn lucky? "Maeve, I ..." He paused, unsure of what he'd been about to say. He wanted to tell her that she was everything, but the words got stuck in his throat.

"Me too, Ben." She raised her hand to beckon him closer.

He took hold of it and put one knee on the mattress. He leaned over her and brushed a few loose strands of hair away from her face. "No regrets."

She smiled up at him. "No regrets."

When their lips met this second time, he kissed her

slowly. Tenderly. Maeve wasn't a woman you rushed with, no matter how badly your body might be urging you to. You took the time to savor every bit of her.

She sighed, and arched her back to give him better access. Ben coasted a trail of kisses down her neck to her chest, still dewy from the rain. He licked the droplets from her skin, and she shivered. He continued his downward descent, and when he placed a wet, open-mouthed kiss over her breast, Maeve moaned.

"I need to feel you," she said, sitting up and tugging her dress off over her head. His clothes followed, and then his eyes drank her in—every curve and valley—before he went back to worshipping her with his mouth.

"That feels so good," she breathed out, her Irish lilt becoming more pronounced.

"You're so beautiful," he whispered as he moved down her body. "You drive me wild."

"You too," she answered, tangling her hands in his hair. "The first time I saw you—"

Her words died on her lips when Ben's mouth crested the rise of her belly and ventured south. "The first time I saw you," he said, picking up where she'd left off, "I thought you were the most beautiful woman I'd ever met." His finger slipped inside of her and she gasped when he found her clit. "And I told myself if I ever got to do this with you, I was going to do it right."

Her hips bucked forward and he sank deeper. "I want you so bad, Ben."

"Me too, Maeve." His muscles bunched as he went to rise from the bed to grab protection. Her hand on his wrist made him freeze.

Her eyes found his and their gazes held. "I'm on birth control. And clean."

His breath caught in his throat and his heart kicked against his chest. He couldn't be sure, but it might have stopped beating for a few seconds at the implication of those six words.

Up until now, if you'd have asked Ben if he'd had good sex, he'd have said of course. Now, he wasn't so sure. Because whatever this was with Maeve was unlike anything he'd ever experienced. It wasn't about two people using the other's body to get off. They had a real connection, one he hoped would last a lifetime. Being with her meant something. He couldn't say what, but he knew it was a shifting point in his life: before Maeve, and after. And they hadn't even made it to the main event yet.

"I'm clean too," he said slowly. The trust she was putting in him blew his mind. "Are you sure?"

She nodded. "If I only get to have this with you this one time, I want all of you."

So that was exactly what he gave her. Twice. And when they finally drifted off to sleep several hours later, Ben knew he'd never be the same.

13

Waking up next to Ben was far too easy.

Maeve held her breath for a moment as she registered the warm body curled against hers, one long arm thrown over her waist with a hand tucked under her hip. His slow, even breathing warmed her neck, sending wisps of her hair tumbling across the pillows. A tumult of emotions washed through her with the clarity of morning light peeking through the curtained window of her bedroom. She'd slept with Ben. She'd done a hell of a lot more than sleep with Ben, actually. She'd had the best sex of her entire life. Twice. And there was a ridge pressed firmly against her backside that indicated there might be another round coming, if she was up for it.

Was she up for it? She let her breath out slowly and tried to analyze her feelings. Was Demi Lovato right? Was ruining their friendship worth it? What if she'd ruined everything by finally throwing herself at him? The mix of humiliation and despair and sheer horniness that had sent her tumbling into his arms wasn't anything to be proud of. She winced. She'd had to talk him into having sex with her. He was a damned good friend, apparently.

"I can hear you thinking." His voice was low, sexy, and sleepy. "You should stop." His arm moved, slipping from under her hip to travel along her belly and explore her breasts. When his fingers found her nipple, her brain went blank as electricity shot through her from head to toe. Shivering, she rolled over to face him and he slid his hands up into her hair, pulling her toward him and capturing her lips in a long, devouring kiss.

Somehow, before she knew what was happening, he'd rolled her further until she was on top of him, the blankets falling away as the tip of his cock brushed the sensitive skin at her center. Gasping, she stared down at him. He was smiling up at her, the same warm, sunny smile he always had, though his eyes were heated as they roved her body in time with his caress. When he grasped her hips firmly and nudged, she rose slightly at his direction, aligning their bodies. She threw her head back as she sank down and he filled her, allowing all thoughts of friendship and the future to slip away as pleasure chased through her veins.

Ben borrowed her shower for a quick rinse, and came back smelling like the Irish soap her mother sent her every month. It gave her a dizzying sense of familiarity as he leaned over her to kiss her forehead.

"Are you okay?" He paused. "Are we okay?"

She nodded. "Still friends, right?" She looked up at him, nerves jangling as she waited for his answer.

Unfortunately, all of her concerns had came roaring back with a vengeance while he'd been in her bathroom.

His smile was easy. "Still friends."

"Nothing's changed?" Her world had been rocked, but she could deal with it. Probably.

His smile stayed in place, although something seemed slightly different about it. She couldn't quite identify what it was. "Nothing."

She sat up, keeping the sheet over her breasts even though it seemed silly given that Ben's hands and mouth had been all over them not even ten minutes ago. Her nipples were still hard, even though her body was lax. "Now what?"

He crossed his arms over his chest as he stepped back to make room for her to get out of the bed. "You tell me, Maeve." Something that looked like pain flickered across his face, but it was gone before she could process what it might mean. "I don't want to lose what we have. I told you that."

She felt her cheeks heat with embarrassment. "You mean before I jumped your bones?"

He laughed. "I promise you, the bone-jumping was mutual."

They both knew she was the one who'd pulled him into this confusing situation, but he was too nice to admit any of that. It was one of the things she adored about him —his unwavering support and kindness. The least she could do was take a step back and try to get them on even footing again.

"So. No more, then." She rose from the bed and reached for the robe that hung carelessly over a corner of her dresser nearby, shrugging into it before she looked back up at him.

He was nodding. "We got it out of our systems, right?"

Fat chance. Her system was flooded with him. She craved him more with every second. But that wasn't so different from how she'd felt before, was it? Unfortunately, now she knew exactly what she was missing.

She blew out a breath as she cinched the robe around her waist. "Yeah. Out of our systems."

He relaxed. She hadn't realized he'd been holding his body so stiffly. "Great. Listen, I have to get to work, but I'll text you later, okay?"

She nodded, not trusting herself to speak, and walked with him to the front door. There was a long, awkward pause while they decided whether they ought to hug, kiss, or shake hands. Finally, he snaked one long arm around her for a sideways hug and pressed a kiss to the top of her head while she tilted desperately toward him like a flower seeking sunshine. Then he was gone, striding down the walkway to his car.

Maeve's forehead thunked against the door as she watched him through the peephole. God, she was an idiot. She'd practically forced her best friend to have sex with her, declaring that she didn't care whether it ruined their friendship. He'd *told* her he didn't have many close friends, and because of that, he valued what they had intensely. No matter what either of them said, she knew perfectly well that their friendship wasn't going to stay the same.

She'd ruined everything, just because she'd had a shitty date.

Her train of thought was interrupted when she realized that Ben had stopped dead on the sidewalk in front of her house. He was standing still, shaking his head. His back was still to her, so she couldn't see his face. She looked behind her automatically, wondering if he'd forgotten something. She was pretty sure he'd taken his phone and his keys. She swung her head back around to peer through the peephole and found herself face-to-face with Ben. He was back on her doorstep, jaw set and brows drawn down as he knocked firmly.

She gave herself the space of two breaths before she opened the door. No sense letting him know she'd been watching him walk away. That wasn't what friends who were totally okay and not at all affected by earth-shattering sex did, right?

He started talking as soon as the door was open. "I lied."

"What?"

He set his hands on her elbows and propelled her backwards into the house, kicking the door closed behind them. "I lied, Maeve. I can't do it."

Her heart sank. "Can't do what?"

He let go of her and ran his hands through his hair, blowing out a sigh. "I can't go back. It's like we let some kind of genie out of its bottle." His gaze roamed over her. "A really sexy genie."

She couldn't help but let loose a small snort of laughter. "A sexy genie? That's where you're going with this?"

He waved his hands airily. "I'm not a master of metaphor, Maeve. I'm just a man who really, really wants you. Again and again and again." His voice dropped to a low murmur at the end of his statement, and he moved in close, pressing her back against the wall of the hallway. He tilted his head forward and rested his forehead against hers. She could feel his breath warm against her lips.

She swallowed. "So what do you want to do?"

"Ruin the friendship," he muttered.

"We did that pretty thoroughly." She bit her lip. "I'm sorry. I didn't mean to change everything."

His lips trailed down her cheek and rested lightly against her throat. "I want to take you out."

She blinked. "What?"

He raised his head, and she almost whined at the loss of his warmth against her skin. "On a date, Maeve."

She stared blankly at him. "A date?"

He nodded. "A real one." His lips twisted slightly. "One that starts and ends with the same person, even."

"I thought you just wanted—"

"Sex?"

She nodded, hating herself for a moment. When had she become this helpless woman who was willing to toss everything out the door for a man—even this man—to get her naked?

"Don't get me wrong, Maeve. I'm certainly hoping the night heads in that direction." He offered her a rakish grin and trailed his finger lightly along her waist, making her shiver through the robe. "But I really, really want to spend time with you. Clothed." He paused. "I mean, mostly."

"But—"

"We have fun together, right?" She nodded, and he continued. "So isn't it possible we could have fun together as more than friends? I mean, I've never done it before, but I hear it's possible to have a relationship with somebody you actually like."

"A relationship?" she squeaked. Something in her brain stuck on the 'never done it before' part, but she shook it aside in favor of freaking out about the more immediate prospect.

His arms fell away from her, and he stepped back, looking uncertain. Her heart ached with a physical throb at the expression on his face. "I mean, if you don't … if you're not—"

"I am," she said. "I do. Want to go out with you. It just … seems too good to be true." She bit her lip.

"Well, that's flattering." He grinned at her. "Might want to reserve judgement until you actually go out with me, though."

She smiled. "I mean, I've been out with you plenty, technically." They'd met up for all sorts of things lately. And she'd always had fun. The idea of going out with him on purpose, romantically, sent anticipatory shivers down her spine. How much more fun could they possibly have?

His jaw dropped. "Wait. Have we been accidentally dating this entire time? Max is going to kill me."

This time she let out a real laugh, from deep in her

belly. "Definitely not. If we have, we wasted a lot of time getting to last night."

His heartfelt "God, yes," made her giggle. Then she sobered as he twined his fingers through hers. "So we're doing this? We're trying it? Going out on a limb?"

"If your idea of a date is climbing trees we're going to have a problem," she said.

"Not that kind of limb, you nerd." Affection warmed his voice. "And I think I can come up with something you'll like."

She raised her eyebrows. "That sounds like a challenge."

"Nope. A promise." He wiggled his fingers at her. "Rooooomance."

"I can't wait." She leaned in, relishing the idea that she could just kiss him anytime, no awkwardness or weirdness involved. Dating was way better than friendship. Assuming it worked out, anyway. She chased that thought away as his lips met hers. She'd already ruined their friendship. What was the worst that could happen now?

14

A week later, Ben reached into the fridge and pulled out two beers. Grabbing the bottle opener, he popped the cap off of both and strolled into Max's living room.

"Thanks," Max said, leaning forward to take the bottle of local cult beer from his hands. He'd just put in a full week at Frankie's, and today was his one day to relax.

"Don't thank me. You're the one with the rare beer hookup." Ben fell back onto the couch, his body sinking into the deep, soft cushions. So much better than the lumpy futon in his small apartment.

Everything about Max's house was so much better, in fact. The living room was a temple to all things masculine, including a top-of-the-line seventy-inch high-def TV, a stereo system that could shake the walls, two different gaming consoles, and a sectional that sat approximately fourteen grown men for Sunday football.

In a quick moment of weakness, Ben missed his old condo in San Francisco. He didn't necessarily miss his old life in the city, but it hadn't been easy giving up all of his fancy belongings when he'd sold the place fully furnished to a twenty-three year old tech millionaire.

Max pushed to his feet with a groan, interrupting Ben's walk down memory lane, and stretched his arms high above his head. His spine popped audibly. "The guys'll be here soon. I should get the chili started." Noah, Sean, and Iain were coming over later for their regular poker night.

Across town, Angelica, Naomi, Jess, and Maeve were binge watching *The Gilmore Girls*. Or at least that's what they said they were doing. Ben knew differently, though. Maeve had confessed to him a couple of weeks back that they only got through one episode before a second bottle of Noah's wine was opened and Lorelai and Luke's on-screen relationship was replaced with talk of real-life relationships. Their last gathering had been especially uncomfortable for her, since Naomi had decided to share some pretty explicit details about how talented Iain was with his tongue.

He chuckled, remembering the horrified look on Maeve's face as she'd explained that no sister ever needed to know what her brother was like in bed.

Briefly, Ben's mind flashed back to all the wicked ways he'd used his tongue on *her*. Would Maeve tell her friends about their night together? He raised his beer to his lips as he considered how he felt about the group knowing they'd taken their friendship to the next level. He figured Naomi would be supportive; after all, she'd been pretty vocal at Frankie's about wanting him and Maeve to hook up. The conversation had been horribly embarrassing for the both of them, but he found it hard to wish it had never happened. After all, it had ultimately led to her begging him to come inside her house ... and then inside her, too.

"You have that look on your face again." Max set a platter of various canapés and dips on the coffee table in front of Ben.

Ben blinked and glanced up, hoping he didn't look too guilty. "Sorry, was just thinking about some things." He reached out and popped a mini red bell pepper coated in a bacon cheese dip into his mouth.

"About Maeve?" Max's hands were planted firmly on his hips and his lips were turned down in a scowl.

Ben understood Max's need to protect young women who weren't the best at protecting themselves, but Maeve wasn't Isabella. Hell, she was the furthest thing from Max's sister. Isabella floated through life—jumping from one dead-end job (and man) to the next—while Maeve had her feet firmly planted on the ground. The woman ran her own freaking distillery, after all.

"Look, man. I get that you want to protect Maeve, but she's not your sister."

His friend bristled. "I never said she was."

Ben set his empty beer bottle on the table and pushed to his feet, clapping his hand onto Max's shoulder. "No, but you're doing that overprotective big brother thing with her, and you don't need to. Maeve's a big girl, capable of looking out for herself."

Max raised a skeptical eyebrow. "Yeah? Then what was that scene at Frankie's all about? Seems to me she doesn't have the best taste in men."

Ben tried not to wither under Max's pointed stare. Surely his best friend didn't put him in the same category as a douche like Steve Smith.

Ben grabbed his empty bottle off the table and headed toward the kitchen, Max falling in line with him. "She made a mistake," he explained, even though he felt he shouldn't have to. "I seem to recall you making a few of them over the years, too, but you don't see anyone trying to protect your virtue."

Max groaned. "Point taken." Not too long ago, Max had been close to asking a beautiful, wealthy divorcée to marry him, only for her to run off with her ex-husband's richer best friend, leaving Max with an expensive diamond ring and a broken heart. Since then, he'd seemingly sworn off relationships, settling for quick flings with locals who knew the score and tourists he'd likely never see again.

"All I'm saying," Max continued, "is that I've been your friend practically my whole life, and outside of high school, I can't name *one* woman you've ever been serious about. Admit it, you're kind of a player. And like I said before, Maeve's not someone you fuck and run on. She's the type of woman you marry."

"I'm not going to fuck and run." How could he convince Max that he'd changed? You'd think the fact that he was still in River Hill instead of back in San Francisco—or New York, Boston, or Seattle—proved he wasn't the same guy he'd been once upon a time. It wasn't as if he hadn't had ample opportunity either; he had an inbox full of inquiries from big name firms all over the country wanting to fly him out for interviews. But the thought of going back to that life didn't seem as enticing as it once had.

He had a theory as to why that was, but he didn't want to investigate those feelings too closely. Regardless, he knew deep in his bones that wherever this thing with Maeve was going, he'd never been the type of person to lead someone on the way Max was suggesting. Time to hit back.

"And the fact that you think I'm capable of doing something like that to someone as special as Maeve says more about *you* than it does about me."

Max's jaw flexed as he bit back whatever retort he'd been about to toss out, and his eyes flicked to the window where Noah, Sean, and Iain could be seen making their way up the walkway to the front door of Max's mid-century modern house. "This conversation isn't over," he said, his gaze bouncing back to Ben's.

Ben disagreed. "Yes, it is. Maeve's a grown woman, and I'm a good guy. Maybe I haven't always been one, but I've changed, Max. If you can't see that, I don't know what I can say to make you believe it."

The doorbell rang, interrupting their discussion. Max stared at Ben for a beat and then nodded brusquely. "Okay, then. If you say you've changed, you've changed." He brushed past Ben, stopping briefly to squeeze his shoulders, before moving to let the others in.

When Iain shook Ben's hand a minute later, he tried not to look guilty for the things he'd done to his younger sister the night before. He didn't have anything to hide, but if Maeve hadn't liked hearing how Iain and Naomi spent their nights together, he was doubly sure the affable Irishman wouldn't be quite so affable if he was treated to a play-by-play of Ben's night with Maeve. One he hoped to repeat again soon.

"Wait, explain that again?" Ben took a bite of his hot dog as Maeve pointed out the various positions on the field. Several stories below, Ireland played Australia in an exhibition match meant to increase interest in rugby in the U.S.

Back when he'd first started working in the city, Ben had known a few guys who'd played for a club in San Francisco, and he'd been to Kezar's with them a couple of times to watch the big international matches, but he'd never seen anything like this in person. The men on the field were massive, making the guys Ben had known look like middle schoolers. He was pretty sure one of them was legitimately seven feet tall.

And he didn't even want to think about how banged up they'd be the following day. He winced and rubbed the bruise on his thigh he'd gotten when he'd accidentally banged into the small dining table in his apartment on the way to the bathroom last night. He was fit, and in good shape, but he knew beyond a shadow of a doubt that he was not cut out for the gladiator-style shit taking place below them.

"G'wan, Declan!" Maeve jumped to her feet and pointed at the field as a man in a green number ten jersey streaked past a mob of defenders and toward the end zone. Err, the try zone. He was still getting the hang of all the new terminology she'd tried to teach him on the drive down from River Hill "Help him out, lads!" she hollered, which was immediately followed by an angry roar. She threw her hands up when the player she'd been cheering for was tackled and the ball bounced out of his grip and into the hands of a waiting Australian. To her apparent relief, the Aussie was immediately tackled and the ref blew his whistle, signaling the end of play.

Maeve dropped back down into her seat and let out a long sigh. "He had no support." She was speaking to him, her Irish accent as thick as he'd ever heard it, but her eyes had stayed glued to the field, her face red and her hands balled into tight fists on her knees. Her shoulders were up around her ears, and every muscle in her body was strung tight as she followed the action below.

Watching her, Ben wondered if he'd made a mistake in getting the tickets for their date. He'd seen them on Craigslist for a steal, and had thought giving Maeve a taste of Ireland would be a nice treat, but now he wasn't so sure. His kind, sweet Maeve was an entirely different creature here. While he'd seen her lose her temper twice with their friends, he'd never seen her this worked up.

It was ... kind of arousing, come to think of it.

He had a feeling it was a side of her most of their friends, save her brother, hadn't ever seen. She was the nice one, the do-gooder who tried to see positivity in every situation. And because of that, people often thought she was naive. She wasn't. She was just a supremely decent human being. One with a tough streak a mile wide when it came to rugby, apparently.

"Get him!" she shouted when the Australian fullback

made a clean break, only to get crunched between four Irish players before being flattened to the grass. "Yes!"

A couple of seconds later, the game was halted while medics made their way onto the field to treat a serious gash over his eye that had coated the front of his jersey in bright red blood.

He glanced at Maeve, who had a wide grin on her face. As if sensing him staring, she turned to him and raised her eyebrows. "What? That guy's a homophobic cunt who shouldn't even be allowed to play given the shit he spouts on social media."

Ben felt his smile growing wide. "You're amazing."

She did a double take. "What, why? That's just common decency."

He chuckled, and shook his head fondly, lacing their fingers together. "You're fun, Maeve Brennan."

She smiled at him and then dragged her attention back to the field. But instead of pulling her hand away, she leaned closer and rested her head on his shoulder as she watched the rest of the game unfold.

In the grand scheme of things, a date to a rugby match wasn't a huge deal. And sitting here with her hand twined with his was the most innocent thing in the world. And yet, it *was* a big deal. Max hadn't lied when he'd said that Ben hadn't been serious about anyone since high school. Hell, he hadn't been in a real relationship since he was sixteen and Maisie Wagner had broken his heart right before homecoming. He'd almost forgotten how good it could feel to simply hold hands with someone you cared about, how ... right. Yeah, that was the word. Everything about him and Maeve felt right.

He just hoped he knew how to make it last.

A cheer went up and Maeve surged to her feet, bringing him with her. "Whoooo!" she hollered as Irish players jumped into each other's arms and slapped one another on the back. On the pitch and in the stands, players and fans alike celebrated Ireland's win over Australia.

Maeve tugged on Ben's hand. "Come on. I have a surprise for you." She bounced on the balls of her feet, barely able to contain her excitement.

"Oh yeah?" he asked as they inched their way down the row to the exit.

She nodded. "Yup."

He pulled her out of the aisle and into a cinder block alcove, wrapping his arms around her waist. "What kind of surprise?"

"Remember when I said my family is one of the team's sponsors?"

Ben nodded. Sometimes he forgot that Maeve came from money. Brennan's Irish Whiskey was to spirits as Guinness was to beer, and yet you'd never know it by looking at her. Dressed in jeans and a long-sleeved black cotton shirt with an Ireland scarf draped around her shoulders, she was the very picture of casual.

She shuffled closer and smiled up at him, her green eyes twinkling in the glow from the stadium lights. "It turns out sponsors get a suite at the hotel down the street."

Ben tried to hide his surprise. On the drive there, she'd mentioned that she was glad he didn't have work the next day, and Ben had *hoped* that meant she was going to invite him to spend the night when they got back to River Hill. Apparently, she had other plans.

"Oh yeah?"

She nodded. "I talked with my oldest brother this morning. It's ours if we want it." She glanced away, suddenly shy.

Ben fingers bracketed her chin and he guided her face back around. Leaning forward, his lips hovered enticingly over hers. "Oh, I want." And then he kissed her soundly, proving to her just how badly.

15

They stumbled giggling into the hotel room, and Ben stopped dead, making Maeve bump into him. She peeked around his broad shoulders to see what had surprised him and grinned. "That sponsor life," she teased. "It's pretty good, eh?"

He blew out a breath. "You're telling me. Here I was just going to take you home and hope you'd let me in the door. You're kicking it up a notch, woman."

She laughed. The suite was gorgeous. She'd taken advantage of the perk once or twice before, although not recently. This particular room was definitely one of the nicer ones she'd been in. A crystal chandelier hung over their heads, lighting the way down a short hallway that opened up into a living area decorated with plush sofas and an armchair that made her want to open a romance novel and dive into it immediately. Champagne was chilling on the small dining table by the panoramic window that overlooked the city's lights flickering off the water of the bay. She headed toward it. "Bubbly?"

"Sure." He prowled through the room, running his hand along the upholstery of the furniture. "But then let's check out the important room."

"Oh, you mean the bathroom?"

"Very funny." He pretended to glower at her. "For all you know, I need a nice hot bath after all that yelling."

She felt her face heat. "I get a little excited about the game."

"So I noticed." He came closer to her, eyes darkening. "I especially liked when you encouraged the Irish team to murder their opponents."

"I—"

"I never knew you were so bloodthirsty." He captured her waist and tugged her towards him. "I like it."

"You do?" It came out in a squeak, and she cleared her throat. "You do?" Her second attempt wasn't much better.

"Oh, yes. Maeve Brennan's dark side. She seems so nice. Until you know…" he paused dramatically. "Her deep, dark secret."

"Wait, what's my deep, dark secret?"

"Um, your inclination toward murder, obviously." He rolled his eyes. "I'd be in fear for my life if I played rugby."

"It's a good thing you're safe." She giggled. "I have other plans for you."

"Ooo, I like the sound of that." He dipped his head forward and kissed her thoroughly, leaving her breathless when they finally parted. "Thanks for showing me your dark side."

"Thanks for buying the tickets." She laughed. "You brought this upon yourself."

"I'm glad I did." He wrapped his fingers around hers and tugged her away from the table. "Let's go check out that other room."

"Good plan," she murmured, distracted by the feel of his hand on hers. When he touched her, it felt like she'd been covered in snow that was rapidly melting in warm spring sunshine. She wanted to melt all the way. "The bedroom it is."

They made their way through the suite, champagne forgotten, and paused in the doorway to the bedroom.

"Good god, this room is made for sex." Ben said it reverently, nearly whispering, as though they'd stumbled upon a hidden temple.

Maeve couldn't help but agree. The bed was the biggest she'd ever seen, dwarfing the king sized one her brother owned. She'd once been on a tour of a historic castle back in her school days; the bed here was oddly reminiscent of the one that had been in the lord's bedchamber.

While the fabrics in the living room of the suite were cool, beachy blues and grays, here in the bedroom it was all reds and soft browns. Most of the space was taken up by the giant bed, while a door to the bathroom was tucked off to the side. Next to it was a built-in gas fireplace mounted high on the wall, a long, slender rectangle filled with quietly flickering flames. A raw-edged wood mantle held a few candles, an ornamental dish, and a pair of solid crystal tumblers with a matching decanter full of what looked like it might be bourbon. And underneath that—Maeve's eyes widened as they fell on the large faux-fur rug. It was more than big enough for two bodies, and she felt a shiver run through her at the idea of being under Ben, her back pressed into the downy softness.

She glanced at him, and realized that he was watching her. His eyes flicked between her and the rug, and he raised one eyebrow. His smile was slow and wicked. "Having some thoughts?"

She swallowed. "Maybe a few."

"Me too."

And then his hands were on her, and somehow her shirt was gone, and her fingers were clawing their way underneath his shirt to find his satin skin. His mouth fastened on her nipple, sucking gently through her bra until she was whimpering. His only response was to let her pull his shirt over his head as he switched sides to give the same attention to her other breast.

She arched her back as he slid a finger around the clasps of her bra. Her breasts, now unconfined, flattened against his bare chest and she hissed in a breath at the vibrant contact. His mouth moved to her throat, nipping lightly, and she retaliated by working her fingers into the waistband of his pants. She slid her fingers as far as they could reach, working her way through silky hair to brush against the base of his cock. It was his turn to suck in a breath. She grinned.

"You're overdressed," he muttered.

"So are you."

"Mmm. Planning to do something about it?"

She tightened her grip and he let out a quiet moan. "Maybe."

"God, Maeve." He slid his thumbs into her jeans and

yanked them down over her hips without bothering to unzip them, dragging her panties with them. She kicked them off and reluctantly let go of him to return the favor. The second his jeans hit the floor, his arms were around her waist and he was picking her up and lunging toward the bed.

She laughed as he practically threw her down onto it. "Was there something you wanted?"

"You, Maeve. Always you." He stared down at her, and she stopped laughing. His eyes were heavy-lidded, his pupils dilated with desire.

She reached up and pulled him to her. Their lips met, and she opened to the soft pressure of his tongue. His hands were everywhere, and hers weren't far behind. She managed to get a solid handful of his perfect ass before he shifted, dragging his fingers down her side and over her thigh. He found her clit, circled it with precision, and she spared a moment to thank any deity she could think of that he was far better at this than he was at making coffee.

Then all thought was lost because his fingers were in her, and his mouth was on her, and she was riding a wave of pleasure that crested as she gasped his name. His fingers disappeared momentarily, but before she could protest, they were replaced by something much more satisfying as he slid inside her. He pressed deep and paused, both of them breathing hard. They stared at each other, and then Ben bent and kissed her again, their tongues tangling and breath mingling. And then he started to move, and she lost herself to the moment.

Pressure built, and she arched underneath him as he

grabbed her hips and shifted both of them to a new angle. When he thrust home again, she barely held back a scream. He kept going, strong and steady, as he managed to hit every single pleasure center she possessed on each upward stroke. When his mouth found her nipple and bit lightly, she saw white light behind her eyes as she exploded into wild pleasure. She clutched his shoulders, digging her nails in, and rode out her orgasm as he slammed into her twice more before shuddering her name and thrusting wildly as he came long and hard.

The second time, they moved to the rug, and Maeve thought she'd never come so hard in her life as she did with the whispery tickles of the rug against her skin and the warm heat of Ben above her. He leaned his forehead against hers, still inside her, both of them breathing hard. She didn't want him to move, wanted to keep him over her and in her and all around her forever.

"I'm going to buy one of these rugs," he whispered. She felt herself tighten around him involuntarily and he jerked a little, both of them shuddering through aftershocks brought on by the thought of doing this again and again. She didn't know what exactly was in his head, but she imagined the two of them on a giant fur rug in the middle of her living room and couldn't help but let out a little moan.

Eventually, they made it back to the bed and collapsed together in a tangled pile of limbs. When she woke up, he was curled around her, her head pillowed on his arm and his lips pressed against her shoulder even in sleep.

She breathed deeply, taking in the scent of sex and Ben, and smiled. Snagging the suite had definitely been a good idea. When he'd told her that he'd gotten tickets to see Ireland play, she'd been ridiculously charmed by his thoughtfulness; she'd mentioned liking rugby maybe once in passing. That lawyer brain of his was like a steel trap, apparently. He remembered everything from her favorite coffee order to her least favorite pair of shoes.

Speaking of his lawyer brain ...

She twisted within the circle of his arms and rolled to face him, discovering him watching her sleepily.

"What are you thinking about?" he murmured.

"Youth Mentors." She answered honestly, without thinking.

He raised an eyebrow. "We're naked in bed and you're thinking about your volunteer organization? I thought I did better than that."

She snorted out a laugh. "If you do any better I won't be able to walk for a week. I was thinking about you, and your sexy brain."

He looked faintly amused. "You think my brain is sexy?"

She nodded. "Of course I do." She shifted, tucking herself closer in to him, and his arms tightened around her. "Tell me honestly; do you think the motion you filed will work? Will the developers back off?"

He nodded. "Yeah. I threw the kitchen sink at them. And I know what I'm doing, Maeve. I don't mean to brag, but I always get my man. So to speak." He smirked, and something in her belly twisted unexpectedly. His tone was oddly similar to Steve's when he'd talked about 'closing the deal,' just one of the many red flags about the other lawyer she'd ignored.

But Ben wasn't like that, she told herself. Ben was good, and kind ... *and the exact same kind of corporate lawyer*, her annoying brain reminded her. He'd admitted himself that he'd never been on the same side as places like Youth Mentors. He'd always been the bad guy.

Maeve shook her head. She had to trust him. She'd *already* trusted him. He'd proven himself over and over again, and she didn't need to worry. She didn't dare think too far into the future, but nobody who made love like Ben did could possibly be a bad guy. Her legendary bad luck streak with men was finally over. It had to be.

16

It was barely ten o'clock in the morning, but already Ben was dragging. Maeve had secured a late check-out from the hotel, but instead of heading back to River Hill, he'd taken her to dinner at his favorite ramen restaurant in San Francisco's Outer Richmond district. Afterward, they'd driven out to Ocean Beach to watch the waves roll in until the wind coming off the Pacific had chased them back to his car. He'd finally pulled into his driveway around midnight, and when it came time for sleep, he'd sorely missed the luxurious bed back at the hotel ... and Maeve curled into his side while in it.

When his alarm went off five hours later, Ben had wanted nothing more than to turn it off and go back to sleep. Unfortunately, he had a job to do, and on Monday mornings that meant arriving at The Hollow Bean at a quarter to six for his eight-hour shift.

Ben's dry, scratchy eyes flicked back up to check the time on the clock once again. While the two days he'd spent with Maeve had been worth it, he knew it wasn't something he could make a habit of. Assuming, of course, he continued working as a barista—something he grappled with more and more every day. He'd taken the job here as a stop-gap while he figured out what to do with his life, but the time was quickly approaching when it could no longer be considered temporary.

Unfortunately, he was no closer to knowing what came next today than he'd been when he'd arrived in River Hill four months ago and knocked on Max's door. With a sigh of resignation, he admitted it was probably time for him to revisit the most recent batch of emails he'd received from headhunters. He knew for certain he didn't want to go back to a firm like Baker, Thompson, and Keene, but that didn't mean there weren't other jobs out there more suited to his ambitions.

Which begged the question: what *were* his ambitions these days?

Ben's manager cleared his throat loudly. "You going to stand around daydreaming all day, or are you going to give that man his coffee?"

Ben felt his ears turn pink with embarrassment. That was the other thing. He'd been doing this job for months, and while he was no longer the disaster he'd been on that first day, he also hadn't ever gotten very good at it. And he wasn't used to anything less than excellence. "Sorry. Coming right up."

He finished making the no-foam soy latte and turned to pass it to the waiting customer but his hand halted midway over the counter. Standing across from him was a smirking Steve Smith. The bruise from where Ben had punched him had faded to a mottled yellow with faint purple shadows near the bridge of his nose.

"Barista-slash-lawyer." Smith scoffed and shook his head. "You know how pathetic that sounds, right?"

Ben ground his teeth together to prevent himself from saying something that could potentially bring his manager's wrath down upon him. Some days it felt like Rodney was just waiting for him to fuck up so badly that he could fire him on the spot. He couldn't give Smith the satisfaction of being the one to add the final nail to his coffin.

"Here's your latte." He pushed it the rest of the way over the counter.

Smith grabbed hold of the to-go cup, but instead of leaving, he eyeballed Ben with a speculative gleam.

Ben had seen that look once before—back at Frankie's, right before the other man had wrapped his arm around Maeve and tugged her in close to his side. It was a little bit knowing and a lot bit predatory.

"I looked into you after you left my office the other week. Quite the fall from grace you've had." He raised one eyebrow.

Ben was pretty sure it'd been waxed and sculpted into that high arch.

"That's nice," he responded. *Do not engage. Do not engage. Do not engage.* "Have a good afternoon." Ben hoped the guy would take the not-so-subtle the hint and get the fuck out of there.

He didn't. Instead, he rested his hip against the counter and set his coffee down next to him, adopting a pose that indicated he was settling in for a nice, long friendly chat. Ben stifled an impatient groan. "Telling your firm's biggest client to go fuck himself wasn't the best move for your career." Smith glanced around the coffee shop meaningfully. "Obviously."

"Is there anything else I can get you?"

Ignoring the question, Smith continued undeterred. "Not smart, but it took giant fucking balls, I'll give you that. Still, probably ruined your chances of getting hired again in San Francisco. Why didn't you just move to another city?" He raised that damn eyebrow again.

"I did. It's called River Hill," Ben answered curtly. He didn't understand where this conversation was going, or why the other lawyer was showing an interest in him. He just wanted the man to leave so he could finish out the rest of his shift in peace. His head was pounding, and he needed a fucking nap.

Smith snorted and rolled his eyes. "You and I both know your talents are wasted in a place like this. That move with the EPA was brilliant, by the way. My boss practically had a coronary when I told him about it. He ranted and raved for a good ten minutes about what a prick you were." He paused and leaned forward dramatically, lowering his voice as if to impart an important secret. "And then he asked what it would take to hire you away from Youth Mentors."

Ben must not have heard him right. It sounded like the developer wanted to give him a job. That couldn't be right. "He did what, now?"

Smith chuckled and leaned away. "You get Youth Mentors to withdraw all their petitions and counter-motions, and Hartwell Properties will set you up with a sweet ass contract in Honolulu, overlooking Waikiki Beach, the land of constant sun and itsy bitsy bikinis."

Ben knew he was tired as fuck, but that made zero sense. "What?"

"I was there on the last project. Six months of absolute bliss, man." Smith smiled wolfishly, as though the two of them had something in common. What he thought that was, Ben couldn't be sure. "You work four ... five hours a day tops, and then you spend the rest of your time trolling the hotel lobby bars for sexy tourists who are in town and looking to hook up with a local. You would not *believe* how many bachelorette parties are there on any given weekend." He waggled his eyes suggestively.

"But you aren't a local," was the first thing that popped into Ben's mind and out of his mouth. Frankly, he was still trying to figure out what the fuck was happening here.

Smith just laughed. "No, I'm not, but they didn't need to know that." Suddenly, he leaned forward, all pretense of joviality gone. "You in or what? My boss needs to know by Friday."

Ben scratched his jaw. "Honestly, I don't know what to say."

Smith slapped an envelope on the counter and pushed it toward Ben. "Well, you'd better figure it out soon, because this offer has an expiration date. You make sure the deal goes through here, and you could be sitting pretty in Hawaii in less than six weeks." He grabbed his coffee and took a few steps backward toward the door. He raised the cup in farewell. "Make the right decision, man. For both of us." Then he was gone.

Ben stood there for several long moments staring at the closed door. His head was pounding, and his mind was whirring. He didn't trust Smith as far as he could throw him, but the offer was compelling, he was forced to admit. A six-month contract could be precisely what he needed to test the waters at a new employer. If he didn't enjoy the work, he could always pack up his suitcase and head back to … where? Portland, and his parents? As much as he loved them, no. That was definitely out of the question.

Suddenly, an image of Maeve standing on her front porch, her mouth split in a beatific smile, popped into his head. In his imagination, she threw her arms wide in welcome, and he dropped his leather satchel to his feet and marched purposefully toward her. He gathered her into his arms and kissed her soundly. He let the daydream unfurl, giving it a full backstory. He'd missed her so damn much, even though she'd visited him in Oahu only three weeks before, but three weeks without seeing her precious face and kissing her delectable lips had been just about the extent of what he could handle. They'd spent the first twenty-four hours of her visit holed up in a bedroom overlooking Diamond Head before venturing out to explore the island for the next two days. When she'd left, it had felt like she'd taken a piece of his heart with her. But the separation had been good, too. It had given him time to figure out what he wanted to do professionally, while replenishing the bank account he'd depleted while working as a barista. Now he could move back to River Hill and be the type of partner Maeve deserved. Someone who didn't live above his best friend's garage in a three-hundred-and-fifty square foot studio that became unbearably hot when the temperature soared above seventy degrees. Someone who was her equal.

Splat.

Ben was pulled from his daydream by the sound of a wet towel being slapped down onto the counter next to him. His eyes flicked between it and the red face of his boss.

"That's it, Worthington," Rodney said, spittle flying from the corners of his mouth as he glared at Ben. "I've given you a million chances because I respect the hell out of Max, but I'm done. I need employees who know what the hell they're doing, and that's not you. Bobby's been trying to get your attention for the last five minutes, but you're standing there staring out the window like some lunatic while you pour milk all over my goddamn floor." He pointed angrily at Ben and then at the tiles at their feet.

Ben's gaze followed, landing on an empty quart of milk in his left hand. "Shit!" All thoughts of Maeve and his career pushed to the furthest recesses of his mind, he tossed the empty container into the trash can and picked up a crumpled wad of towels. Throwing them down onto the puddle, he dropped to a crouch and began wiping up the mess.

After a few seconds, Rodney's hand fell onto his shoulder. "Don't bother. Just go."

Hesitantly, Ben rose to his full height, a good six

inches over his balding manager. He swallowed deeply. "Go?"

Rodney nodded and stuck out his palm. "I'm gonna need your apron, son."

Ben stared at him for a beat, trying to process what the fuck had just happened. One minute he was making coffee, the next he was getting fired. Again. And somewhere in the middle, he'd apparently been offered a job that could be the answer to all his problems.

If only it wasn't working for the company that's trying to ruin the organization you're currently trying to save, his conscience reminded him.

Yes, if only.

Ben slowly lifted the apron off over his head and passed it to the other man, trying to work through his shock. "I'm—"

"Save it," Rodney interrupted. "You were never cut out for this job, Ben, and we both know it."

And that was the crux of the situation, wasn't it? The only thing Ben knew how to do was be a lawyer—the type that ran point on corporate takeovers and hard-fought negotiations. He'd turned down his nose at Steve Smith, but they were more alike than Ben cared to admit. Sure, he wasn't a complete sleazeball like the other man, but at the end of the day, they were cut from the same corporate cloth. Maybe it was time he accepted the truth and moved on. After all, there were worse places in the world than Hawaii.

He pushed the doors of The Hollow Bean open and stepped out into the bright spring afternoon. The historic town square was filled with moms pushing strollers, old men walking their happy little dogs, and little old ladies sitting together on park benches knitting. In the gazebo, two people were being instructed on how to waltz. Everything—from the bright pink tulips dotting the brick pathways to the colorful banners advertising the upcoming spring festival—was picture perfect.

No, Honolulu wasn't bad, but neither was River Hill. Too bad he couldn't seem to claw out a real future here.

17

Maeve shut the door of her car and leaned against it in the driveway of The Oakwell Inn. She stretched, feeling her muscles loosening and her body relaxing. After a long night and day with Ben—followed by an even longer day at work—she really should be getting caught up on her sleep. But a meeting of River Hill's super secret romance book club was not to be missed.

Angelica had inadvertently started the club when she'd made Naomi read some of her beloved historical romances. Maeve and Jess had joined later on, and now she relished the infrequent meetings—they could only meet when Angelica's inn wasn't booked, which was rare these days. They probably could have gathered at any of the other members' houses, but Maeve and Jess's places were too small, and Naomi was weird about people being in her house. Iain lived there, too, but Maeve rarely visited her brother at home. They saw each other plenty at work and with their friends. So now, whenever

Angelica had a free night, the romance bat signal went up, and they gathered here at The Oakwell to discuss their latest read.

Maeve slung her green canvas messenger bag over her shoulder and patted it warmly, feeling the outline of the paperback inside. This month, they'd read a book about a woman who'd discovered that the supposedly spam emails she'd been receiving from an African prince were the real thing, and she was actually an actual modern day princess. Reading about the heroine balancing love, royal duties, and her desire to have a career in public health had been a joy—and the sex scenes had been great, too.

Maeve grinned slyly as she headed for the front door. For once, the steamy scenes in the books they read had nothing on her real life sexy times. The smirky smiles that Angelica and Naomi—and even Jess, lately—exchanged whenever the subject came up had been pretty grating until she met Ben. Or rather, until she'd gotten naked with him. Being "just friends" had done a number on her vibrator. Thank goodness that drought was over.

"Knock knock," she called as she pushed open the unlocked door. "Anybody home?"

"I'm not," Noah said, appearing in the doorway to the kitchen. "Ignore me, I'm on my way out."

"Not joining our discussion?" she teased.

"I'll email you my thoughts." His tone was dry, and she laughed.

"I look forward to it."

"You should; I'm very witty."

"Stop congratulating yourself and get out," Angelica said from behind him. "If you're not here to talk about romance novels, you're not allowed to be here."

"I read the book," he protested, to Maeve's great surprise. She'd assumed he was joking.

"But you don't want to talk about it." Angelica's hands were on her hips, her brows drawn down into a frown that almost looked real.

"Only to you. Preferably in bed." He leaned forward and kissed her, then hoisted his leather folio under his arm. "Got distributor contracts to review tonight, and you don't want to listen to me talking about that, either."

Maeve raised her hand. "I do."

He shot her a quick grin. "Don't go poaching my distributors, you whiskey maven."

"It's a completely different market! We could share!" Her fingers itched to see what was in his folder.

"I'll keep it in mind." He eased past her, holding the bundle high over her head. Noah Bradstone was a very tall man, and built rather like the side of a mountain. He easily evaded her, and she stuck her tongue out at him as he went out the front door.

"Call Iain, at least!" she shouted after his retreating backside. "He's very generous!"

"I'll say." Naomi's purring voice came from behind her, and Maeve turned to find the artist leaning casually against the archway that led into the front parlor, where they usually gathered for these meetings.

Maeve held up her hand. "Whatever you're thinking about is definitely not what I'm talking about." Ignoring Naomi's satisfied grin, she stalked past the other woman into the parlor and sank down onto one of the antique upholstered sofas. The last time they'd all gotten together —for *Gilmore Girls* night, a ritual where they let the show play in the background while they gossiped about each other and the town in general—Maeve had managed to avoid discussing what had happened with Ben, while Jess had waxed poetical about married life and Naomi had made gagging noises until they'd all been clutching their sides and gasping with laughter. Naomi and Iain were happily *un*married, and as far as anyone could tell, they intended to remain that way in perpetuity.

Maeve had stopped discussing the matter of her brother's love life with her parents—even though they brought it up about every other phone call. The Brennans had two other sons, both married with children, but their father frequently badgered Iain to "make things official" in front of a priest back home. Frankly, Iain's relationship with Naomi seemed far healthier than their older brothers' did, so Maeve couldn't understand why their father refused to accept it as it was.

The slam of the front door distracted her from her thoughts, and she looked up to see Jess flying through the foyer carrying a stack of magazines and heading for the kitchen. Curious, Maeve rose and followed her.

"These are the ones you asked for." The pile of magazines slid out of Jess's arms to land haphazardly over the kitchen island's Carrera marble countertop.

Despite not having a background in design, when Angelica had renovated this place, she'd done a beautiful job. The Oakwell Inn frequently appeared on the cover of both lifestyle *and* home renovation magazines. Of all the rooms here, the kitchen was Maeve's favorite. She paused in the doorway as she almost always did, admiring the sunny space in front of her. While it looked like it had sprung from the pages of a magazine, the exquisite décor was made warm and welcoming by the fresh flowers scattered in vases throughout the room and bottles of Noah's wine littering the countertops. In addition to the tasting room at the vineyard next door, the couple frequently hosted tastings and other events here. Maeve made a mental note that she should do the same. What was the use in having a friend with a perfectly-styled B&B if you couldn't sell your whiskey there?

She strolled further into the room to examine the magazines as Angelica began to gather them up. *Oh.* Bridal magazines, all of them. "What are these for?"

"Planning my wedding," Angelica said, giving her a strange look.

"Oh. Oh, right." Maeve flushed. She'd forgotten that Noah had finally convinced Angelica to set a date after Jess and Sean had surprised them all by eloping to Costa Rica.

"And when you're done, they'll make lovely kindling for the fire pit," Naomi said.

"You can be as snarky as you want about it as long as you'll design the invitations and menus," Angelica told her.

"Of course I will." Naomi held her hand over her heart. "I'll even give you a reduced rate. You know, for love."

"What a delight you are," Angelica said dryly. "I'm so glad we're friends."

Naomi grinned. "Me too." They exchanged blown kisses and chuckles.

"Are we ready to talk about the book?" Jess asked. "Because I loved it. And I neeeeed to talk about some of those scenes." She waggled her eyebrows so her friends would know exactly which ones she was referencing.

"Grab the Chardonnay out of the fridge," Angelica directed. "I conned some snacks out of Max, too."

"Does anyone pay for anything in this town?" Maeve wondered.

"Coffee," the other three women chorused.

Maeve grinned, and finally dropped her bomb. "Speak for yourself."

"What?"

"Really?"

"Tell!"

Maeve found herself driven back toward the parlor under an avalanche of shrieked inquisition. Laughing, she held up her hands in self defense. "I thought we were here to talk about the book!"

"I'll brain you with the book if you don't spill!" Angelica waved her purple-covered copy threateningly as they all settled into their seats.

"It's possible I may have spent some quality time with River Hill's finest barista," Maeve said as modestly as she could manage.

Naomi snorted. "River Hill's worst barista, you mean." By now, everyone had had a chance to try Ben's services at The Hollow Bean.

"Trust me, his coffee making skills were the last thing on my mind," Maeve told her.

"Last night?" Jess squeaked.

Maeve shook her head. "Two nights ago. He took me to a rugby game."

Two blank looks greeted her and she turned to Naomi for help. "Surely you've gone."

Naomi nodded. "Iain and I went last summer when the Irish 7s were in town for that big tournament. He got the suite—ohhhhhh." Her voice trailed off and she pinned Maeve with an accusing glare. "You didn't."

"I did."

"Naughty girl."

"Very," Maeve said smugly.

"Can somebody fill me in?" Angelica asked, looking between them.

"The Brennans sponsor a rugby team," Naomi explained. "One of the perks of said sponsorship is the use of a very swanky hotel suite for any family members or high level executives who attend the matches. Since only Maeve and Iain are in America to make use of it ..." She looked away guiltily, and Maeve wondered if the whole idea of nepotism was something Naomi still struggled with. It had nearly been the undoing of her relationship with Iain back in their early days.

"Wait, you had hotel sex for your first sex? That's setting the bar pretty high." Jess giggled.

Maeve felt herself flushing. "It, uh, wasn't the first time we'd had sex."

More shrieking ensued, this time accusatory. "When?!"

"You didn't tell us!"

"What's the first rule of romance book club?"

Maeve sighed. "Sex scenes come first."

Angelica shook a finger at her. "And that includes our personal lives."

"I know, I'm sorry!" Maeve tucked her feet up under her on the sofa and accepted a glass of wine. "The first time was after that date at Frankie's."

"When he took you home? I knew it!" Jess whooped. "I told Sean he was going to make a move that night."

"Um, I made the move, actually." Maeve's cheeks heated again at the memory of her desperation. Thank God it had worked out.

"You jumped him?"

"Oh, yeah. Invited him in, never let him leave." She shook off the bad part of the memory and grinned at Naomi. "I thought it was going to be a last hurrah for our friendship but in the morning he asked me out."

Angelica bounced in her chair. "Tell us about the sex! The sex is the important part!"

Maeve laughed. "Does Noah know how much you tell us?"

"Sean makes suggestions," Jess said. "He says he wants to sound good for posterity."

They all laughed. Bolstered by the wine, Maeve let a few details slip.

"I think I need to get a big fur rug," Angelica said dreamily.

"Do you think they sell them in bulk?" Jess asked.

Naomi was the only one who seemed unmoved. She was watching Maeve with an odd expression on her face.

"What?" Maeve asked.

"What made you sleep with him?" Naomi asked bluntly.

"Um, have you seen him?" Maeve gestured with her glass in a vague approximation of Ben's Captain America-like physique, nearly spilling her wine on the sofa.

"Yes, and you insisted on being just friends with him for ages—which included going out with somebody else." Naomi's brows drew down into a small frown. "Did you sleep with him just because you were lonely?"

"No!" Maeve sat straight up and set her glass down on the coffee table. "No. I mean, I was. Some. But also he's… great. Really great. Kind, and sweet, and supportive. Interesting, too."

Naomi's lips thinned. "You know what he did for a living before he became a shitty barista though, right?"

Maeve opened her mouth to defend Ben's coffee-making skills, then decided not to bother. "Yes. He was a lawyer."

"A serious shark, Maeve. I Googled him." Naomi bit her lip. "I used to know a lot of guys like him, back when I still hung out in my parents' circle. Serious corporate types."

"That's not him anymore, Naomi."

"Really? You think being a barista is going to keep a guy like that happy forever? Has he ever said he plans to stay here? Have you talked about the future at all?"

"Naomi, relax," Angelica said. "They've had one date."

"And a lot of sex," Jess piped in helpfully.

Maeve frowned. "Are you ever going to support anybody I choose to be with?"

The other three exchanged glances and she found herself exhaling through sudden pain in her stomach, as though someone had punched her.

"It's just…we're concerned," Angelica said gently.

"The last one—"

Maeve interrupted Jess with a sharp movement of her hand, as though she were karate chopping the memory of Steve Smith away. "The last one was a mistake. We all know that. It doesn't mean I have indiscriminately bad taste in men!"

"Nobody's saying you do," Naomi said sharply. "What I'm saying is that corporate sharks don't lose their teeth, Maeve. Don't get bitten."

It was far too late for that, Maeve thought. Her blood was already in the water. If Ben was circling to devour her, he could have her.

But was Naomi right? She'd blithely assumed their friendship would translate into a relationship that was on its way to becoming permanent. But now that she stopped to consider it, he'd never said he planned to stay in River Hill. And with the first inklings of dread, she recalled how happy he'd been to get his lawyerly mojo back when he'd started working on the Youth Mentors case.

Suddenly, she wondered if she was just a stop on his road back to shark-infested waters. In that moment, she felt like a very, very small fish in a big, dangerous ocean.

18

"Hey, babe." Ben laid a quick kiss on Maeve's cheek as he stepped into her house and moved toward the kitchen at the back. In his left hand, he held a six-pack of beer he'd pilfered from Max before heading over, while in his right, he carried a bag filled with all the fixings for a barbeque for two.

It was probably a bad idea for him to have spent so much on the two ribeyes now that he didn't have a job, but he'd needed to do *something* to make himself feel better after getting fired the day before. Gorging himself on local, grass-fed beef seemed a hell of a lot smarter than drowning his sorrows in his girlfriend's whiskey. Although now that he thought about it, he might want a bottle of it when he explained to her that he was once again jobless.

"Ooh, what's that?" she asked, following him into the room.

He broke two of the cans off their plastic holder and passed one to Maeve before crouching down to root around in the refrigerator to make room for the rest. "Max's friend did a collaboration with another brewery, and he dropped off a case last night to get feedback." He popped to his feet and opened his can with a satisfying *hiss*. Swallowing down a few mouthfuls, he held the can out to inspect the label while the flavors settled on his tongue. "Not bad."

Maeve took a drink of her own, smacking her lips together lightly. "Is that lavender? And ... chamomile? Yeah, definitely chamomile."

Ben laughed and twisted the can around to show her the brewer's notes. He'd never get over how *good* she was at things like this.

A couple of weeks ago, they'd been hanging out with Max, watching an episode of *Top Chef* since one of his friends was competing. For that episode's 'Quickfire' challenge, the cheftestants were blindfolded while being timed to see how many flavors they could correctly identify. On the spot, the group had decided to test Max the same way using the nuts and spices he had in his kitchen. Then Max had challenged Maeve to see just how good her supposedly refined palate was. In the end, she'd surprised them all by identifying two more than he had.

"I should have known you'd get it with just one sip."

She shot him a look of mock indignation. "Of course I did. My palate is extraordinary," she said with a wink.

He set the can to the side and wound his arms around her waist. Pulling her between his legs, he dropped a kiss on her forehead. "Everything about you is extraordinary."

Her eyes flicked upward, and their gazes locked. Neither of them spoke for a few protracted seconds.

"Have I mentioned lately how much I like being able to hug you like this?" She sighed happily and nuzzled her cheek into his chest, her arms banding around him tighter. "I used to sit on my hands when I was around you because I was afraid I'd unconsciously reach out and just grab hold of you."

Ben smiled and caressed her hair, letting the fiery strands sift softly through his fingers. God, he loved her hair. Warmth washed over him as the thought flitted through his mind. It settled in his limbs, and radiated inward, suffusing his heart with a feeling of … rightness. In that moment, Ben realized it wasn't only her hair that he loved. He was *in love* with her, too.

He hadn't meant for that to happen—had actively fought against it, in fact, knowing how unsuitable he was as a long-term partner for someone as successful and driven as Maeve—but somewhere along the way, he'd lost control of the situation. If he were being honest with himself, he'd probably fallen a little bit in love with her that first night they'd met … when she'd indignantly dragged him out of The Oakwell Inn, declaring that she was going to take him home and have sex with him.

He chuckled lightly, but the laughter died in his throat. With Maeve tucked snugly into his side, he'd nearly forgotten what a shit show the rest of his life currently was. If he'd been worried before about being good enough for her, now he was doubly so. He'd just been fired. A fact he hadn't yet shared with her.

"What's so funny?" She lifted her head and glanced up at him curiously.

"Nothing," he said, brushing a few wayward strands

of hair from her brow. "I just … I really like you, Maeve Brennan."

She smiled sweetly at him, her eyes turning misty. "I really like you too, Ben Worthington." She canted her head to the side and studied him intently. "Hey, what's wrong?"

Ben blew out a long gust of air and loosened his hold on her.

As if sensing his unease, Maeve took a step back and wrapped her arms protectively over her middle. "Is everything all right?"

He looked up at her kitchen ceiling, trying to find the words to explain. Honestly, the only thing to do was to just spit it out. He met her gaze head-on. "I got fired yesterday."

"What?" She scrunched her eyebrows into a deep vee and pursed her lips. "How come?"

He looked away. He didn't want to admit that while he'd gotten better at his job since she'd had to send back whatever sludge he'd tried to serve her, he'd never really gotten *good* at it. The whole thing was too humiliating. "I think we both know that I was never really cut out to be a barista. They only gave me the job because Max called in a favor."

"What happened? I mean, why'd they fire you now?"

Ben reached blindly for his beer, and when his fingers locked on the cold can, he lifted it to his lips and chugged down several gulps. When it was nearly empty, he wiped his mouth with the back of his hand. "I spilled milk."

She coked her head to the side and her lips tilted up

in a sly grin. "I know this is horrible, but I really want to make a joke about crying over spilt milk."

Despite his apprehension over admitting *why* he'd spilled the milk, Ben felt his cheeks lifting in a rueful smirk. "Yeah. I had that thought too."

Maeve stood tall and pushed her shoulders back. He watched as she forced a grin to her face. "But like you said, you weren't going to be a barista forever. Now you can focus on what you really want to do." She looked at him expectantly.

He recognized this was the point in their conversation where he should tell her what that was. If only he knew himself.

"About that ..." He blew out a long, slow breath. He didn't know if he was trying to buy time or what, but suddenly he was very worried how the rest of this discussion was going to go. "Hey, let's go sit down." He reached out to lace their fingers together and then led her over to the oversized velvet sofa in the living room. It was way too large for the space—taking up nearly the whole wall—but Maeve had told him that she'd loved it on sight and had been determined to make it work in her tidy little house.

She settled her body down into the soft, downy cushions and pulled her legs up under her. She turned to him, her brow furrowed. "I'm trying to convince myself that a guy doesn't show up at your house with expensive steak when he's going to break up with you, but the look on your face ... You're not breaking up with me, are you, Ben?"

Ben scratched his cheek. "No, I'm not breaking up

with you, Maeve. But you … gah. This shouldn't be so hard." He pushed to his feet and paced the room.

She twisted her hands in her lap. "What's going on?"

He stopped and faced her. "I have a lead on a job." He shoved his hands into his front pockets and rocked back on his heels.

"Oh. That's good, though, right?"

"It's in Hawaii."

"Ah."

"Yeah. Ah. And uh …" Ben slapped his palm to the back of his warming neck. "And, um … it's with Hartwell."

Approximately two seconds passed before Maeve's face morphed from confusion to recognition. "What?!" She shot to her feet, swaying slightly with indignation. She scowled and stomped over to him, stretching out a finger and poking him in the chest. Hard. "I *know* you didn't just tell me you're considering going to work for the corporate thugs who are trying to destroy the very fabric of this community."

"Maeve, come on. I need a job; they offered me one. It's not the most unreasonable thing in the world to—"

She shook her head. "I know you're not this stupid, Ben. You have them up against the wall, and they think they can get you to back off with the promise of …" She narrowed her eyes. "What *did* they promise you?"

Ben's neck prickled with guilt. She wasn't wrong about the offer; of course it came with strings and stipulations. That was just how things worked in his world.

His world. The words echoed loudly in his conscience, promptly followed by Max's warnings not to get involved with Maeve if he intended to go back to his old life. He didn't want to be *that* guy, but he didn't know if he could be *this* guy, either. He loved living in River Hill, and he liked who he was with these people. Fuck, he *loved* who he was when it was just he and Maeve. She'd breathed life back into him when he'd wanted nothing more than to lick his wounds and stay hidden forever. But *this* Ben had just been fired again, and not from some high-powered gig either. He wasn't even capable of holding down a shitty job where he made no money. *This* Ben was a loser.

And frankly, he was fucking tired of losing.

"It's a chance for me to feel useful again, Maeve." He went back to pacing the room. "You said it yourself; I wasn't going to be a barista forever, and I have literally no other skills. All I've ever wanted to be was a lawyer. I could do the job for six months and then—"

"Then what? Then you throw some little old lady out of the house she was born in? The house her kids were born in? Do you even hear yourself? How can you stand there and act like this—" She slammed her mouth shut and rolled her lips tightly between her teeth until they formed an angry white slash across her red face.

Ben had never seen Maeve truly angry before. His heart ached with the knowledge that he was the cause of it now.

Her chest rose and fell with deep breaths for several long seconds before she shook her head and then turned silently on her heels. She marched to the front of the house, and when she reached the front door, she flung it open and stalked through it, slamming it loudly behind her.

Ben stood there, listening to the echoing silence of her absence and wondering just what the hell had gone wrong. He'd known this wasn't going to be an easy conversation, but he'd sort of hoped they could discuss the pros and cons logically, maybe make a decision as a couple.

He shook his head as reality set in. He could see now that he'd been kidding himself. There was nothing reasonable or rational about the way he felt about Maeve, and there was no world in which she would have supported him taking a job with the same people who employed Steve Smith. Honestly, he couldn't really blame her. Her unwavering sense of right and wrong was one of the many things he loved about her.

He had no right asking her to approve of him doing something that was so completely anathema to who she was. He'd let a momentary lapse in judgement—which was more like a months-long lapse in confidence—ruin one of the best things that had ever happened to him. He might have lost his career when he'd moved here, but he'd gained the love of his life.

One who was angry and disappointed, and had maybe just broken up with him. He shouldn't have expected anything less. Maeve felt deeply, and with her whole heart. A job was just a thing he could do to make money. Maeve, however, was *the one*. Everything else was secondary. Which, obviously, she didn't know. She hadn't given him a chance to tell her.

A renewed sense of purpose propelled him toward

the door. When he was halfway there, it burst open, the knob hitting the wall and bouncing away.

An angry Maeve strode through like a tiny, vengeful Valkyrie and pointed outside imperiously. "This is *my* house. You should be the one to leave."

He moved toward her, but she held up a staying hand. "Naomi was right. Sharks don't change their ..." She shook her head. "Never mind. Shark, tiger, whatever; it's all the same. You both sense blood and go in for the kill. I'm not going to be prey anymore."

"Maeve, I—"

She thrust her arm toward the door. "I said *leave*."

"If you just let me explain—"

"You've said enough." She gave him her profile, her chin raised. "Please, go."

19

Maeve had no idea how she'd gotten to work this morning. She'd spent most of the night after Ben had left crying and scribbling furious, incoherent notes on how to save Youth Mentors herself. Not that she'd be able to once Ben rescinded all of the legal work he'd done before jetting off to Hawaii. Hartwell would steamroll them.

She glanced at the wad of notes she'd shoved into her bag on her way out the door, and then snorted and crushed them into a big ball of yellow paper. She threw the wad toward the wastebasket next to her office door and missed. Somehow, that made the tears flow all over again, and she buried her face in her hands.

How could she have been so stupid? Angelica and Naomi were right. She had terrible taste in men. For all of his pretty words, Ben had been happy to drop the case that meant so much to her as soon as he was offered a plum deal.

Despite her unhappiness, her conscience forced her

to be fair and admit that he'd been fired. Again. And was probably worried about money. But surely there were other options he could have pursued instead? Coffee shop work was clearly out, but if he wanted to return to law, there had to be other firms. Ones that weren't actively trying to destroy everything she knew and loved.

Her rational side pricked again, pointing out that little bit of hyperbole. Youth Mentors was a valuable part of the community, but her life would hardly fall into some sort of post-apocalyptic dystopia if the organization wasn't around. *Ugh.* Her practical side sounded far too much like her father's voice in her head.

Maybe she'd overreacted. Ben was an adult. He needed a job. Her mind traveled down the pathways of what had happened last night, arriving at logical destinations until it slammed sharply against the fact that his job offer was from Hartwell Properties. She could handle him getting fired—he really was a fairly terrible barista. Nor did she begrudge him wanting to be a lawyer again. He'd proven how good he was at it. She could even forgive him wanting to go back to corporate law, though the idea left a bad taste in her mouth. Maybe he could find a way to only work on projects that benefited the communities they were in?

Which brought her back around to him working for this specific developer. Ben knew first-hand what they did, the sorts of projects they took on. And he hadn't said it outright, but she had a strong suspicion that the job offer was conditioned upon him withdrawing his support of Youth Mentors, dooming the organization and striking a terrible blow to the kids they worked with. She couldn't understand how he could think she'd want him to work there. She couldn't understand him wanting it, either. Not the Ben she'd fallen in love with.

Because damn it all, she *was* in love with him. Helplessly, hopelessly, head over heels in love. With the man who'd made her the worst cup of coffee she'd ever had. Who'd followed her out of The Oakwell Inn and laughed with her about her outrageous insistence that they'd be having sex. Who'd blown her bloody mind when they finally did have sex, over and over again. Who'd been proud of her success, and fascinated by her skills, and supportive and demonstrative and kind at every turn. She'd fallen in love with *that* Ben, and she didn't know how to stop loving him when it turned out she didn't really know him at all.

She raised her head, feeling the stretch of skin stained by salty tears. Grimacing, she dug in her bag for a tissue. She hadn't bothered with much in the way of makeup this morning, but the bare swipe of mascara she'd managed was probably utterly wrecked by now.

"Maeve?" Iain stood in the doorway, and when she looked at him, his eyebrows rose swiftly and he stepped inside, closing the door behind him. "What's wrong?"

She sniffed. "I'm fine." Her hand closed around the packet of tissues and she pulled one out to try to repair some of the damage.

"You look like a drowned raccoon," he said bluntly.

What a delight it was to work with one's brother. She glared at him and rubbed at her eyes with the tissue.

"You're just spreading it around." He crossed his arms and stared at her. "Now you look like a zombie. Possibly an improvement over the raccoon, but as far as I know it's not Halloween, so why don't you tell me what's going on?" He crossed over in front of her desk and pulled out the small chair she kept in the corner for visitors, slinging his body into it like he was utterly relaxed. His cheekbones stood out in tense contradiction of his body language, however, and his jaw was clenched tightly and his eyes glinted with something hard. He might be an easy-going sort of man, but when someone messed with his family or those he cared about, Maeve knew he could be as harsh as their father.

"It's just man trouble." She tried to sound dismissive. "You don't want to hear about it."

"Au contraire, ma soeur." Iain's French accent was terrible. "Naomi may have mentioned some concerns."

"Well, you can congratulate her for being right yet again." Maeve knew her voice sounded bitter. She couldn't help it. Everyone else got to be happy, and here she was yet again feeling alone and stupid. "He has a job offer."

"Oh?"

She nodded. "Did you hear that he got fired from the coffee shop?"

Iain's expression remained completely neutral, something she would never be able to manage. "I may have heard something to that effect." He coughed. "It's, uh, a small town."

"Tell me about it." She rolled her eyes.

"So he's at loose ends?" Iain looked thoughtful, though she didn't know why.

She laughed without any actual humor. "Hardly. He's

off to Hawaii, to go destroy lives in the sunshine and play on the beach afterwards."

"What?" Now her brother looked genuinely confused.

"The damned developer offered him a job—the ones trying to get Youth Mentors' building torn down." She didn't often swear out loud, but just thinking about Steve Smith and his horrible employer made her want to scream obscenities that would make a sailor blush.

Iain was silent for a moment. "Did he take it?"

She opened her mouth, and then closed it, staring at her brother. "I—"

Iain rolled his eyes. "Do you even know?"

"No, he didn't actually—" She flushed. "I threw him out of the house." Conflict-averse Maeve seemed to have vanished lately. She was starting to miss her old self. Little Miss Never Argue might have been a bit of a Mary Sue, but at least she hadn't known what heartbreak felt like. Although she wouldn't have recognized love if it bit her on the arse, either. She wasn't sure which was better. Or worse.

"Maeve."

She scowled at her brother. "Why wouldn't he take it? He hasn't got a job here, or anything to tie him to this place, and they're offering to send him to Hawaii and give him buckets of money to do what he loves to do."

"He's got you," Iain said gently.

"Yeah, well, apparently I'm not enough." Maeve felt tears stinging her eyes again.

"I don't think you should assume that until you hear it from him," Iain said. "And if that's true, I'll punch him in the mouth. And then Naomi will shiv him with a chisel. Sculptors have very strong hands."

She smiled through her tears. "Sweet, Iain, but it doesn't matter. He's on his way out the door."

"It sounds like you sent him on his way without actually listening to what the man had to say. Find out if he's taking the job before you complete your transition to full zombie." He gestured at her eyes, his tone impatient but still kind.

"And if he is?"

Iain sighed. "If he is, I'll be surprised. I'll be honest with you, little sister. Naomi has her doubts, but they're based on some of her own experiences, not necessarily on Ben, the actual person. He strikes me as a man who's a lot different than the person he used to be, and someone who's struggling with the transition into living the life he wants to lead." He paused. "You know, you and I have always had a pretty significant safety net. I don't think he does."

She shook her head. "I don't know that I'd call living with Da any kind of safety. He'd drive me absolutely mad in days. I can barely hold a civil conversation with him on the phone."

Iain snorted. "And you're the nice one. Imagine how the rest of us feel." He sobered, and leaned forward. "But that doesn't change the fact that he's there, Maeve. And so is Brennan's. If all of this failed—" he waved his arm around, encompassing her office, the distillery, and the life they'd both built here. "—we'd have choices."

"Ben has choices," she said stubbornly. "He could choose to not be an asshole."

"I think he's trying to," Iain said dryly. "You just have to give him a chance to do it." He sat back in his chair and rubbed his chin, scratching lightly at his neatly trimmed beard. "You know, we could use somebody to help us with our contracts."

"That's your job," she said automatically. Iain handled virtually all of the administrative work for Whitman's, although his real gifts lay in marketing and sales. He'd sold their whiskey to restaurants and bars up and down the west coast, and recently he'd been making inroads into the East Coast markets, too. Naomi had been snarky about his sales trips until he'd taken her along and managed to sell several of her sculptures to a gallery in Washington, D.C. Then she'd been too busy to complain.

"I know you've been buried in your barrels for the last several months, but I'm assuming you've noticed that our volume is growing." He raised his eyebrows at her and she bit back a snarky remark.

"I have." She'd been working nearly nonstop, not that she wasn't delighted to do so. She'd built herself a fantastic team here, and being in charge of the distilling process herself was a dream come true. She'd spent years working in her father's distillery, fighting a losing battle against the family's resistance to change. When she and Iain had agreed to try to create a completely new blend, she'd been nearly dizzy with the freedom of it. The feeling hadn't gone away since.

"I'd been considering asking for some time with one of the Brennan lawyers," Iain was saying as she pulled herself out of her memories.

She made a face. "Yuck."

He nodded. "Aside from the yuck factor, they're still based in Ireland and I'm making primarily U.S. deals for what's now a U.S.-based brand. Not that Brennan's doesn't have the expertise, but I'd prefer somebody local, you know?"

She nodded, not quite seeing where he was going with this. "So?"

"So you could mention it to Ben," he said patiently.

Understanding bloomed, followed in quick succession by surprise, then hope, then disappointment and a fresh surge of grief. "It's probably too late for that."

He sighed. "You never know, Maeve. He might surprise you. You're worth it, you know."

She didn't feel worth it. She felt battered, broken, and stupid. And possibly a bit embarrassed. Iain was right about the safety net they'd always had. Ben didn't have one; he needed a job. And how could she blame him for wanting his own version of safety? The ease of doing what he'd always done, what he was good at—it was what she was doing, after all. It wasn't as though she'd gone from distilling to being a dental hygienist or something. She'd struck out on her own, but she was still doing what she did best. Ben deserved to be successful again. She couldn't begrudge him that. Despite everything, she loved him too much to want him to be unhappy.

The question was, then, what would make him happy? And was she brave enough to find out?

en hadn't showered in three days. Or something like that, anyway. Honestly, he'd stopped caring about personal hygiene right about the time he'd taken a bite of a hot dog and ketchup had squirted out the end of the bun and splattered his shirt. Instead of getting a napkin and wiping it up like any other civilized man would have, he'd simply lifted the cotton tee to his mouth and licked it clean. Well, cleanish.

He was pretty sure that had happened on Tuesday, and he thought today was Friday. Maybe. He could probably look at his phone to find out, but he'd stopped checking it once he realized Maeve was never going to return his texts, and now the battery was dead. That was probably for the best, though. If his phone *had* been working, there was a very strong likelihood he would have sent her an additional twenty texts to go with the fifteen he'd shot off the day she'd broken up with him.

Ben winced, recalling the moment he'd walked out her front door and it had slammed shut behind him. The reverberation still echoed in his head when things got too quiet. He had experienced some pretty low points this past year, but *that* moment had been the lowest of the low. Getting fired from two jobs was one thing, but getting shit-canned by your girlfriend was on a whole other level.

At this point, he needed a new life plan—it was clear the one he'd been operating from was faulty. The job with Hartwell wasn't an option, not if he wanted to be able to live with himself. Neither were any of the other equally reprehensible firms filling his inbox with offers. But he needed to do *something*. He didn't want to move back home to Portland, but he was forced to admit that living in his parents' house wasn't any worse than wallowing in unemployed misery above his best friend's garage. His brother Nick was doing well out in Maryland. Maybe he could head east to see if he could line up a good job out there. But was living with Nick any better than crashing with his parents? At least if he lived in Portland, he'd get a home-cooked meal out of the deal. Or maybe he could strike out on his own and go some place completely new ... somewhere no one knew who he was or how he'd hit rock bottom. He could start over, build a life for himself.

Except he didn't *want* a new life. He wanted the one he had here, in River Hill. With Maeve.

Which meant he needed to man up, take a shower, and figure his shit out. Not necessarily in that order. He had no idea if she'd forgive him for having even considered the offer in Hawaii, but he had to try. Maeve meant too much to him to give up so easily.

So they'd had a fight. Couples fought all the time. According to Noah, he and Angelica had fought tooth and nail the first six months they were together. And if the things Iain had said during their last poker night were anything to go by, the makeup sex was definitely worth it.

Ben bolted upright.

Shit. Poker night.

If today was Friday, that meant Iain, Sean, and Noah were all over at Max's right now. While his best friend was as clueless as Ben when it came to relationships, Maeve's brother was in a committed, long-term relationship, Noah was engaged to be married, and Sean was a newlywed. If anyone could help him figure out what to do about Maeve, it was those guys. Assuming, of course, they hadn't already decided he wasn't good enough for her.

The thought had him stopping in his tracks on his way to the shower. It was entirely possible that he'd step one foot inside of Max's house and get punched in the face by Iain. Although the affable, laid back Irishman didn't seem like the violent type. Noah, on the other hand? That was more the big man's style.

Ben pushed images of Noah breaking his nose to the back of his mind and yanked his smelly shirt off over his head. He wadded it up into a ball and tossed it across the room into a hamper in the corner. He made quick work of the rest of his clothes and then stepped into the shower, letting the hot water wash away all the stress and stink of the last seventy-two hours. And, apparently, his stupidity, too. Because while he was in there, he had an idea that was so perfect he marveled that he hadn't seen it before.

———————

An hour later, Ben pushed open Max's front door and poked his head inside. "Can I come in?"

Four male heads popped up at his greeting. "I was wondering if you were coming or not," Max said, his gaze dropping back down to the cards in his hands. "I've been texting you all day, and when you didn't answer, I figured you might be too hungover."

Ben stepped over the threshold and into Max's living room where the card table was set up. Settling into a fifth chair presumably reserved for him, he asked, "Hungover?"

Max's eyes flicked back up, his gaze probing. "When I finally got home at midnight, you had that emo shit you used to listen to back in college turned up full blast. I stopped in to tell you to turn it down, but you were passed out on the couch with a pile of beer bottles scattered around you. Didn't you wonder how they'd mysteriously made it into the trash can when you woke up?"

"That bad, huh?" Noah asked.

Ben scrubbed his hand down his face. "I don't even remember that." He scrunched up his nose and looked at the ceiling while he tried to sift through the foggy memories of the evening before. He'd had Chinese food delivered around seven, which he'd proceeded to demolish even though he'd planned to save some of it for leftovers. Then, he'd snuck into Max's house and pilfered a six pack of beer after realizing he'd blown through his own stash already.

Sean glanced up, his gaze subtly probing. He never lectured any of them, but Ben had noticed a time or two that he paid a lot more attention to his friends' drinking than someone who hadn't battled his own demons otherwise would. He was generally nice enough not to say anything, but he sure as hell noticed everything. "Been there, done that, got the t-shirt. Should we be worried?"

Ben shook his head. "I don't normally go on benders, but last night …" He blew out a long breath. "I just wanted to forget the look on her face when she ordered me out of her house. Booze seemed like the quickest way to accomplish that."

"Like I said, should we be worried?"

"No, it's not a problem." He turned to face Max. "And it won't happen again."

"Good," Max said, picking up his poker chips and letting them cascade back into a pile next to him. "I don't want to talk my neighbors out of calling the cops again."

Ben winced. Being arrested for drunk and disorderly conduct or disturbing the peace was all he needed at this stage. Especially if his new plan was going to work. "I'm sorry. Really."

His lifelong best friend tossed his cards into a pile in the middle of the table. "I fold. And it's cool, man. I get it. But you can't say you didn't bring it on yourself."

Without conscious thought, Ben's eyes swiveled to Maeve's brother. Thankfully, the other man wasn't scowling. Instead, his lips were tipped up in a smirk. "If it makes you feel any better, Maeve's just as bad. Christ, the crying is out of control. Thank god Naomi's not like that. I can't handle it, lads."

Ben let out a long, slow breath. As much as he hated to admit it, it *did* make him feel better. He hated that he'd hurt her, but knowing that she seemed to be taking their breakup just as poorly gave him hope. Those tears meant she cared—a lot. And if that was the case, he had a shot at winning back her trust, and, hopefully, her heart.

"Listen," he said to Iain, "I love your sister—" Four pairs of eyes swung to him, and he cleared his throat. "Yeah, I said it."

"Did you say it to *her*?" Noah asked as Iain studied him from across the table.

Ben flattened his palms against the table top. Saying all of this out loud was hard enough, but doing so in front of this particular audience was even more difficult. While he'd gotten to know Iain, Noah, and Sean in the months he'd been in River Hill, he couldn't be sure how they'd react. Each had dealt with their own dramas on their way to happily-ever-after with Naomi, Angelica, and Jess, but this thing with Maeve was different. While she was Iain's family by birth, he'd seen them *all* treat her like a little sister of sorts—and not always in a good way. "No. Not yet. She, um, didn't give me a chance."

"Well, you *had* just told her you were taking a job with her sworn enemy across the fucking Pacific," Iain said, his tone harsh.

Something about the way he'd characterized the situation gave Ben the power to continue. He was a lot of things, but an asshole wasn't one of them. Well, not anymore … and it was important they knew that about him. "Actually, I didn't. I told her I'd been *offered* a job with them. I'd gone over to her house wanting to discuss the pros and cons, but within minutes of seeing her, I knew I couldn't take it. It's not…it's not what I want. No matter how many over-the-top benefits the job came with, I couldn't leave her. I love her."

Iain stared at him for several silent beats, during which Ben swore it was silent enough to hear a pin drop. The older Brennan's lips flattened into a hard line and he nodded once. "Okay, then. What are you going to do about it?"

Ben reached into his back pocket and pulled out the sheet of paper he'd put together before coming downstairs. Slowly, he unfolded it, flattened it, and then turned it around so the other men could see it clearly. "If the work I did for Youth Mentors taught me anything, it's that there isn't a lawyer in town who knows real estate and contract law as well as I do." He pushed the paper across the table. "And that got me to thinking. I don't need to work for some big, fancy firm with a marquee list of clients to find fulfillment. There's enough work right here in River Hill and the surrounding communities to build my own practice. It won't be easy, but how's that saying go again?"

Max grinned at him from across the table with what looked to Ben's eyes a lot like pride. "Nothing worthwhile ever is," he finished.

"Exactly," Ben said. "It took me awhile to see it, but I'm right where I'm supposed to be. I fucked up, I know that, but hopefully when I tell Maeve how I plan to do good for the community, she'll see I'm not the asshole she accused me of being. I want to build a life with her, here. But I'm going to need your help." His gaze swept over the table. "I hate calling in a favor like this, but between you, you know practically everyone in River Hill. And those you don't know, your significant others do."

Noah leaned back in his chair, his burly arms crossed over his barrel of a chest. He glanced down at the paper and then back up to Ben. Slowly, a smile spread across his bearded face. "Max always said you were one of the smartest fuckers he'd ever met. Glad to see you finally realize it, too."

21

There was only so long you could wallow in indecision before life swooped back in to distract you, Maeve found. She wanted to talk to Ben, but she was terrified to reach out to him.. What if he said he was leaving? What if he said he *wasn't*? He'd sent a lot of text messages at first, while she was still furious and capable of deleting them with a sense of righteous indignation. Now she wished she hadn't, because he'd gone radio silent.

She'd tried to hide her misery at work, although she was pretty sure she wasn't fooling anyone. Iain had rolled his eyes at her several times, but they were both too busy for him to deliver another version of his earlier lecture. Orders were rolling in, and she and her team had their noses to the grindstone while Iain was looking slightly frazzled with the effort of sustaining his current marketing push and doing all of the administrative work they needed to stay on top of things. Maybe he was right, and they did need to find a lawyer for the contract work.

It was as good an excuse as any to reach out to Ben, she reasoned. Even if he wasn't going to stick around— her heart hurt at the thought, a physical ache that made her wince and rub her chest—he might know somebody who could help them out. And if he did tell her he was leaving, she could pretend the only reason she'd reached out at all was for work. Unless, of course, he wanted to stay. She couldn't let herself dwell on how much she wanted him to stay, and go back to being the Ben she knew and loved.

She sighed and packed up her bag. She was due at Youth Mentors for a volunteer shift, and she was dreading that nearly as much as she was dreading calling Ben. She hadn't heard anything one way or another about the legal situation. Whether Ben had withdrawn his petitions or not, the organization was still vulnerable, still ripe for the picking for developers like Hartwell. Joan had worked so hard and done so much good for the community; to see her efforts fail simply because her office was in a prime location for development had to be galling. It infuriated Maeve, and she'd only volunteered there for a short time.

She said her goodbyes to the staff at the distillery and drove across town. As she parked her car, her phone buzzed with a text. It was from Joan, telling her that while she was gone for the day, there were a few items to be dealt with on the front desk. Maeve smiled fondly down at her phone. She'd grown to like Joan immensely over their recent acquaintance. Like an older version of Angelica, she seemed to know everyone and everything in town. Maeve wondered what she would do if Youth Mentors went under. Start up another charity? Retire for real? She already played golf with the mayor every week.

Shaking her head, she slid out of her car and headed for the door. It was unlocked, which surprised her. Maybe one of the other volunteers was still here. Normally when Joan left, she locked up behind her and Maeve used her own key to open the place back up. She dropped her bag on the chair behind the front desk, noticing a piece of paper with Joan's handwriting laid over the computer keyboard. It looked like a to-do list.

A thump from the offices at the back startled her, and she frowned. "Hello? Anyone here?"

Another thump and a distinctly male grunt were her only answer, so she headed down the hallway to investigate, reaching the two former classrooms at the back half of the building. One of them was Joan's office, and the other had been empty ever since Maeve had begun volunteering.

Except now it wasn't.

She stopped dead in the doorway, eyes wide, and tried to understand what she was seeing. Ben stood in the middle of the room, behind a large desk that hadn't been there the week before. He was heaving a heavy box from the floor onto the desk with a grunt. It landed with a thump, and she understood the sounds she'd been hearing. What she didn't understand was why.

He wore dark jeans and a plain t-shirt, which clung to his muscles as he shifted the box. His resemblance to Captain America was back with a vengeance. A brief, searing memory of those muscles bunching under her hands as he lifted her into bed made her mouth suddenly dry out.

"B-Ben?"

He looked up. "Oh! I didn't hear you come in. Hi." His smile was warm, friendly, everything she was so used to from him. It confused her even more.

"What are you doing here?" she blurted.

He picked up a boxcutter and began to open the taped box with swift, economical movements. "Unpacking my office."

"Your office?" He was speaking the same language she did, surely, but the words didn't make any sense.

"Yep."

"I don't understand. I thought—"

"That I was off to Hawaii?" He met her eyes, smile still in place but something else in his gaze. Something that looked...determined? "That's not me, Maeve. Not anymore. You showed me that."

She took a slow step forward, finally entering the room and glancing around her. The desk wasn't the only thing that was different. Several bookcases lined the walls, and there were two long filing cabinets underneath the window at the back. A comfortable-looking chair she vaguely recognized as once having been in the parlor at The Oakwell Inn was in front of the desk, and a standard office chair was behind it.

He stood at the desk, one hand still holding the boxcutter, watching her solemnly. "That job in Hawaii, and what they wanted me to do to get it..." He drew in a deep breath, then let it out slowly. "I'll freely admit I probably would have done it, before."

"Before?"

He set the tool down carefully. "Before this. Before River Hill, before you. I was a trainwreck, Maeve." His lips tilted briefly into a small smile before he continued. "I burned out, got fired, came crawling to Max and started doing whatever I could to pay rent. But it was never what I wanted. And it never was sustainable."

She nodded. "I knew that."

"For a while I thought I should just go back and do the same thing again, eventually, once I'd taken a break. And then I met you." He stepped toward her, and she instinctively stepped back. She needed to hear the rest. His face froze, a little bit, but then he swallowed and continued. "You showed me that I'm a different person now."

"I don't—" She swallowed, realizing that she was about to say something she never thought she'd say. "I don't think you should give up the job just for me, Ben." It hurt to say it out loud, but it was the truth. She couldn't be the solitary anchor that weighed him down and kept him here, no matter how much she loved him. Or he loved her. Because he did, she knew it, deep down. He loved her a lot, and it made her feel astonished and delighted and terrified in equal measure. Just like the way she felt about him.

"It's not for you, Maeve." When her eyes flew up to meet his, he actually laughed a little. "Sorry! I'm not saying this elegantly at all. But you're right. You were the catalyst, but I really *am* different. The thought of taking that job made me feel sick, when I actually thought about anything but my bank account."

She frowned. "So what is all this?" She gestured toward the office's new furnishings.

"This is my new life," he said quietly. "One I hope to share with you, if you'll let me."

Her blood thundered in her ears as the world seemed to fade away. "What did you do?"

"I know a lot about the law, you know, and there aren't a lot of lawyers poking around River Hill to help the people here. I asked around, and there's one divorce lawyer working in the next town over and everything else has to go through the internet, or people hire lawyers from Santa Rosa." He stepped back and found his desk chair without looking, sinking down into it and steepling his fingers under his chin as he glanced up at her. "So I'm opening up a practice."

She blinked. "Here?"

Now his grin was practically smug. "I negotiated a lease with Joan that was mutually satisfactory. And has the benefit of making this building home to a for-profit enterprise as well as a nonprofit one, which means it's a multi-use facility that falls under several new codes that are fairly difficult to wiggle around."

"So Youth Mentors—"

"—Has nothing to worry about. And a lot to do, if the way Joan was scribbling notes earlier means anything. She said she was leaving you a list."

She nodded vaguely, her mind still processing everything he'd just said. "Wait. For-profit? Like, you'll be making money?"

"Why Maeve, what a mercenary question." He grinned, and she blushed.

"I didn't mean it that way."

"I know. To answer the question you didn't actually ask, yes, I have a client list already." He held up his hand and began ticking names off on his fingers. "Max wants me to look over some employment contracts and franchising opportunities, Noah practically threw distribution contracts at me, and even Rodney over at The Hollow Bean said he'd like me to go over their lease agreement, because he wants to make some improvements. I suspect there will be more, too. There are a lot of small businesses in this town, and nobody has been around to help them with some of the legal mumbo-jumbo that often stops entrepreneurs in their tracks. I know all the tricks."

She didn't know what to say. What came out of her mouth was, "Iain will want to talk to you about contracts."

He smiled. "He did mention something about it, but he said he wasn't going to commit to offering me a retainer until he knew you were on board."

"You can have it," she said instantly. "I was actually going to call you later." She flushed again, remembering the way she'd dreaded the call. She should have called him days ago. "We definitely need some help as we grow."

"I think I'm the right man for the job." His voice quieted. "Am I the right man for you, too?"

She swallowed, then closed the door of the office behind her and walked over to him. "You are. You always have been." She set her hands on his shoulders and his arms came around her waist as he buried his face against her neck.

"I'm sorry I ever considered taking the job," he murmured, his lips moving against her skin like satin.

"I'm sorry I didn't let you tell me you weren't taking it," Maeve replied. "I'm not usually like that."

She felt him smile against her. "Should I be proud that I'm the only one who can drive you to it? Or scared?"

"That depends on if you do it again."

He tugged her down into his lap, their bodies tangling together in the office chair. "Never. I'm completely reformed."

"Not completely, I hope." She wound her arms around his neck. "There were a few things about Bad Boy Ben that I liked. Especially when he got naked."

"Mmm. That reminds me. You're going to get a package delivered to your house soon."

"Oh?"

"I may have anticipated things a little and ordered one of those fur rugs."

A delicious shiver went through her. "You were pretty sure of yourself, huh?"

"I've been sure I wanted you since the day I met you, Maeve. Nothing's changed, and nothing will. I'm staying in River Hill for me, for the life I want to live. But there's nothing I want more than to share all of it with you."

"Starting with the rug?"

"Honey, the rug is just the beginning." He kissed her, then, and she knew that this was forever. She couldn't wait to get started.

**COMING THIS WINTER: THE CHEF'S
CUTIE**

THE CHEF'S CUTIE
(River Hill #5)

Chef Max Vergaras is at the top of his game, but when
he's suddenly forced to play dad to his orphaned niece,
expanding his culinary empire doesn't seem so important
anymore. What *is* important is proving to the beautiful
social services caseworker assigned to them that he's
capable of raising Mia on his own. Unfortunately, his
precarious position isn't the only thing keeping him up at
night. When he does find time to sleep, his dreams are
filled with images of Elizabeth Teague—a woman so off
limits it's not even funny.

Lizzie Teague has an important job to do, and she can't
get distracted by one case—even if Mia's uncle Max has a
way with food that has her thinking about things that
definitely aren't on the menu. But with her career and
reputation on the line, she has to remember why she took

this job in the first place ... and it certainly wasn't to fall in love with her clients—no matter how lovely the sexy, charismatic chef and his young niece might be.

If Max and Lizzie give in to temptation, they have everything to lose. But what if it's possible to gain even more? What would they be willing to risk when love—and family—is on the line?

START AT THE BEGINNING

Start at the beginning with **THE VINTNER'S VIXEN**, the first book in the heartwarmingly sexy River Hill series.

Welcome to River Hill, where the only thing more intoxicating than the wine is the man who makes it.

With movie roles for "curvy best friend" drying up fast, actress Angelica Travis is happy to leave Hollywood behind to renovate a bed and breakfast in River Hill, the jewel of Northern California's wine country. She's got plans and power tools ready, but an inconvenient attraction to her handsome new neighbor is *not* on the agenda.

Winemaker Noah Bradstone's master plan is right on schedule until construction on the B&B next door threatens his prize-winning grapes. His only choice is to confront his sexy new neighbor, but with her pink toolbelt and quick retorts, she's the single most infuriating woman he's ever met. What's even more infuriating is that he wants her anyway.

Despite their constant bickering, Angelica and Noah discover they have more in common than they initially thought—including an attraction that burns red hot. But when his past and her future collide, they're forced to answer some very difficult questions about their relationship. Can their love survive a pair of shocking revelations? Better yet, can they survive each other?

CHAPTER ONE

Having grown up with a mother who planned the family's annual summer trip based on her astrologer's divinations (excellent ones, to her credit), Noah Bradstone might have developed a healthy respect for the mystic and unknown.

You could think that, but you'd be wrong.

So when the universe—in its infinite wisdom—tried to tell him it was a bad idea to get out of bed that morning, he'd glibly ignored the signs.

The first was when he was yanked out of a perfectly marvelous dream involving himself, Joan Holloway from *Mad Men*, and a bottle of fine Kentucky bourbon by the caustic smell of diarrhea wafting into his bedroom. It turned out that Molly, his sweet brown Labrador retriever, had somehow eaten the entire box of donuts he'd planned to bring into the tasting room later that morning. It was the second time that month she'd eaten something she shouldn't have, which also meant it was the second time he'd had to get down on his hands and knees to scrub runny shit stains out of his antique Turkish rug.

And the second sign?

While knee deep in dog feces, his phone began to ring off the hook. He tossed his rubber gloves into a bucket of murky brown water and checked to make sure his hands were clean before picking up the device. Seven missed calls—all before seven o'clock in the morning. He swiped his finger across the screen and groaned when he saw who'd been frantically trying to reach him.

Noah loved his mother—truly, he did—but with his

thirty-fifth birthday fast approaching and no sign of a wife on the horizon (much less a girlfriend), Bernice Winchester Bradstone, scion of San Francisco society, was becoming *restless*. With Noah's two younger sisters married off to men the family matriarch had practically hand-picked for them, her focus was now firmly placed on achieving the same for her dawdling son. No matter that he'd told her repeatedly he didn't want, or need, her help—in his love life or otherwise. But with the city's famed Founders' Ball weeks away, there was no doubt in Noah's mind that was why she was calling.

Instead of returning her calls, Noah flicked the phone's ringer to silent and made his way to the large walk-in shower in his master bedroom. His day might have started off shitty—*pun absolutely intended*—but he wasn't about to let his dream date with the luscious Miss Holloway go to waste.

AN HOUR later Noah was in his trusty, beat up Ford F-150, making his way down the long, winding dirt drive that separated his property from his neighbor's, when he saw a large plume of dust rising up in the distance. Pushing his sunglasses up, he craned his neck forward to get a better look out the windshield. He tried to make out where the disturbance originated, but it was too far away —he couldn't quite tell if it was coming from his land or old Mrs. Winthrop's. He hadn't scheduled anyone to work in that particular field today and, as far as he knew, the estate was still vacant after his neighbor's death a few months ago.

The closer he drove, the more pronounced the dirt cloud became, until he was less than five hundred feet from where a crew was digging up vines and tossing them in a large discard pile in the middle of the drive.

"Holy fuck!" he exclaimed when he realized what he was seeing. He hit the gas, and tires spun in the dry dirt before finding purchase.

A few short seconds later, Noah slammed his truck to a stop and leaped out of the cab, reaching into the bed to pull out a tire iron. "What the *fuck* do you think you're doing?!" He bore down on the crew with the make-shift weapon fisted in his right hand and rage clouding his vision.

The wine industry was made up of all types of people. Some would give you the shirt off their backs if they thought it would help, while others would smile in your face and then stab you in the back the second you turned away. Still, in all the years his family had been in the business, he'd never heard of someone tearing out someone else's vines.

An older, grizzled man stepped forward and crossed his large, beefy arms over his chest. "And you are?"

"I'm the owner of those vines!" Noah hollered, pointing at the increasingly large pile. "And you have about two seconds to explain what the fuck you're doing on my land before I start bashing some skulls in." He wasn't a violent man. In fact, aside from a couple of schoolyard skirmishes from his days at prep school, he'd never been in a fight in his life. But at that moment, he didn't care that it was essentially one against five, and that each man in front of him had at least forty pounds on him. They'd just destroyed hundreds of thousands of dollars worth of award-winning pinot noir and he didn't have the first clue why.

The foreman raised his eyebrow at Noah as if to ask, 'You and what army?' before turning around and grabbing a clipboard from one of his crew. "You don't look like Angelica Travis."

"Who?" Noah stared at the man. "I don't know anyone by that name. My name's Noah Bradstone and those—" he pointed at the pile "—are my motherfucking grapes, and you're standing on my goddamn land!"

What the fuck was wrong with these people?

"I don't know what you're talking about," the foreman drawled, flipping through page after page. Eventually, he found the one he was looking for and passed the clipboard to Noah. "But I have a work order from Mrs. Calliope Winthrop's estate to clear this plot of land up to the property line so the new owner—that'd be Miz Travis —can widen the drive."

Noah examined the diagram and then tossed the clipboard to the ground, exasperated. "You've got to be fucking kidding me." He kicked at the damn thing and missed.

"Now wait just a minute!" the foreman snapped, picking up his paperwork and dusting it off with one big, callused hand. Stepping closer, he pointed menacingly at Noah's chest as the rest of the crew took two steps forward. "I don't know what your goddamn problem is, but I will not have you strolling up and yelling at me and my crew. I was paid to do a job and that's what I'm doing."

Looking to the heavens, Noah counted to three in an attempt to bring his anger under control. He dropped his hands and faced the other man. "Those schematics are laid out *upside down*." He pointed to the opposite side of the drive. "*Those* are the grapes you were supposed to pull out." And then he pointed at his land—his precious, marred vineyard. "*That* is my land. And what you just did cost me a couple hundred thousand dollars in lost revenue. Those vines in that produce the best fucking pinot noir in the country."

He blew out a long breath and linked his fingers behind his head. Marching a couple of paces away, he tried to wrap his mind around what he should do next. Finally, he turned back toward the foreman. "Look, I know you were just doing your job, but I'm going to need your business card all the same."

The man visibly bristled as his crew muttered behind him. "You can't sue me!"

"Maybe not," Noah answered. "But I sure as hell can sue Mrs. Winthrop's idiot fucking grandkids and whoever drew up those plans. So ... like I said, I'm going to need your name." Noah notched his chin. "And I'll be taking that clipboard with me."

"You'll be doing no such thing!" the foreman responded indignantly, tossing it to a member of his crew.

Noah sighed. "Fine, have it your way." He pulled his phone from his pocket and took a photo of the truck parked on the side of the drive—the one that had a large advertisement for Jesse's Landscaping and Maintenance emblazoned on the driver's side door. "I don't know if you're Jesse or if that's your boss, but one of you should expect to hear from my lawyers. Now, if you don't mind, I'll ask you to kindly get the fuck off my property." Noah bent down and picked up the tire iron before crossing his arms over his chest and staring the other man down.

"Fine." The foreman nodded. "I've got no skin in this game. C'mon guys." He motioned for his crew to follow and then they climbed into his large truck and pulled away.

Standing in a cloud of kicked up dirt, Noah looked over his prized grapes and sighed. He didn't have the first fucking clue what to do now. They hadn't covered this sort of thing at UC Davis. Sure, winegrowers ripped out vines all the time—ones that weren't producing as well as they should be, or to make room for new grapes when one style fell out of favor—but he'd never heard of a situation like this. You just didn't do that sort of thing. Not when a winemaker had everything riding on a certain crop from a particular vineyard.

Like he did.

Clearly the universe was trying to tell him something. Noah just wished he knew what the fuck it was. The day had started out badly, he'd just never expected it to get *this* bad.

With another weighty sigh, he thumbed the screen on his phone and brought up his contacts. Scrolling, he came to the only name he could think of who could advise him on what to do now. He hated making this call almost as much as he hated the idea of having to talk to his mother later on. If there were two people who knew how to push his buttons, it was his mom and his dad, the famous cult winemaker Carter Bradstone.

Noah didn't have a bad relationship with his father, per se. By most standards, you could even say they were close. But when Noah had decided to strike out on his own, some harsh words had been said—from both sides. He loved his father, and he loved the man's wines too; they just weren't the types of wine *he* wanted to make himself.

And what's more, he hadn't wanted to wait years to take over as the head winemaker at Bradstone Family Vineyards, only to be constantly compared to his legendary father. He knew he could never change the style of wines the vaunted family winery was famous for, so instead of taking his 'rightful' spot by his father's side, when he'd turned twenty-five, Noah had cashed in his trust to buy his own vineyards from a winemaker who was retiring. His father had been less than impressed with the idea.

Now, ten years later, Noah's gamble had paid off, but his father still had a hard time treating him as an equal. Or, if not equal, then at least a major player in his own right. No matter what Noah did or what he managed to accomplish, it always felt like his dad would see him as an upstart who'd eschewed legacy and tradition to cash in on consumer whims. Noah knew in his heart that hadn't been the case, and the awards and accolades he'd begun receiving the last couple of years validated his instincts, but where family and business was concerned, sometimes cooler heads couldn't prevail.

Still, there was no one more seasoned than Carter Bradstone when it came to dealing with surprises. While his father had never experienced something *quite* like this, he'd seen his fair share of ruined crops in the thirty-plus years he'd been in business. Noah knew he'd have some valuable advice.

At this point, all was lost—there was nothing he could do to salvage the vines—so he needed to think about what came next. With the runaway success of his last bottling of Prodigy Pinot Noir, he'd built expectations around what he was capable of delivering. Now, except for the liquid that was already bottled and laying down, he had nothing left to deliver. He needed a game plan, and much to his chagrin, that meant he needed someone with more experience.

Bracing himself, Noah dialed his father's number and waited for the man to answer. Taking a deep breath, he swallowed his pride and said, "Dad? It's Noah. I need your help."

WITH HIS DESTROYED vines hauled away, Noah shook Vincent Casilla's hand and wished the man well. "Thanks for helping me out," he said, walking the older man to his car. "I appreciate it."

Vincent shook his head glumly. "Such a goddamn shame. Those vines were at least forty years old."

"You're telling me," Noah agreed with a derisive snort. "Looks like my Prodigy Pinot was the last of its kind."

"On the plus side, kid, this might propel remaining

inventory into rarified air. Once word gets out that these grapes are gone, there's going to be a run on what's left. You know how the collectors get."

Noah *did* know how the collectors got. So did Vincent, having been his father's vineyard manager for the last twenty years. Next to his father, Noah trusted Vincent's insight more than anyone else's. He'd started out as a day laborer when he'd first come to the United States, but Carter had taken Vincent under his wing and taught the man everything he knew about growing grapes. Now the two acted as a well-oiled machine, producing wine that graced virtually every table on the West Coast.

"Which would be all well and good if any of that money ever saw its way back to me."

"True, but you've seen what happens once your wine gets added to one of those lists. You can't keep up with the demand. And trust me, this is going to get out. By the way, your dad wanted me to offer you his press team to get ahead of the news."

"Nah, that's all right," Noah said. "I'll take care of it."

That was another way he differed from his father. While every little thing Bradstone Family Vineyards did was announced via a press release, Noah relied on social media channels to talk directly to the people who cared most about his wines: the customers.

Sure, a press release was good to put out when Robert Parker scored your wine a ninety-nine—but for everything else, he took to Facebook and Instagram. Lord knew he'd taken enough pictures of the day's carnage for the insurance report (and potential lawsuit he was already considering) to write a whole tome about the demise of his beloved grapevines. Now he just needed to make sure he could post without using every expletive in his vocabulary to describe the negligent new owner of the old house next door and the assholes who were responsible.

"Thanks again," Noah added as his old friend climbed into the cab of his own truck.

"Anytime," Vincent offered, his hand hanging out the window in a friendly wave as he drove down the drive, turning at the road in the direction of the neighboring valley and Bradstone Family Vineyards.

Alone with nothing but his thoughts and righteous anger, Noah huffed out a loud breath and ran his hands through his hair. This was *not* how he'd anticipated spending his morning and afternoon, and the day wasn't quite over yet. Right before Vincent had pulled up, he'd made another phone call, this one to cancel a meeting he was very much looking forward to.

While on principle Noah hated canceling meetings, this particular one rankled even more. Naomi Klein wasn't just the artist who designed his bottle labels, she was also one of his closest friends. And a little more, sometimes. They'd been friends since they were kids forced to endure the ridiculous traditions and affectations that came with being a part of the San Francisco elite.

If Noah had hated all the times he'd had to don a tuxedo, Naomi had gotten the worst of it. As her parents' youngest child and only daughter, all of her mother's hopes and dreams for social success had been pinned on Naomi. Her debutante ball had been larger and more grandiose than any they'd seen before or since. Noah acting as her escort for that horrible affair had cemented their friendship forever. Here they were, almost twenty years later, still enjoying each other's company. These days, though, they didn't keep it quite as innocent as they had back when they'd been sixteen.

Not that he and Naomi were a couple—much to his mother's chagrin. Aside from her "advancing age," Naomi was *exactly* the type of woman his parents would love to see him settle down with. After all, she had the right name, pedigree, education, and family connections. But that wasn't the type of relationship they enjoyed. The two were friends first and foremost; they just happened to enjoy each other's bodies every now and again as well. That they'd been able to maintain such an unconventional friendship all these years astounded the rest of their mutual friends, but it worked for them and he'd been looking forward to mixing a little business with pleasure with her this afternoon.

Unfortunately, now he had *other* business to attend to. Namely, driving up to the dilapidated home next door to see if the new owner—this Angelica Travis person—was around so he could give her a piece of his mind.

ACKNOWLEDGMENTS

To our families, for all the reasons.

And to our readers, we love you, and want to thank you
for continuing on this journey with us.

ABOUT THE AUTHORS

Rebecca Norinne and Jamaila Brinkley have been friends for almost fifteen years. Separately, they write contemporary romance and historical fantasy romance; together, they created the enchanting world of River Hill.

In this charming Northern California town, Norinne and Brinkley combined the interests that made them friends in the first place—great food, delicious wine, and a pinch of home renovation—and added in the spicy romance they love.

Rebecca lives in Massachusetts with her husband, and Jamaila lives in Maryland with her husband and twin children. They text each other a lot.

ALSO BY REBECCA NORINNE

The Rocky Cove Series

Not Quite Perfect

A Perfect Mistake

Second Time Around

The Dublin Rugby Romance Series

Coming Home

First Comes Love

Just For Now

Take A Chance On Me

Forever At Last

The Billionaire Series

The Contract

The Boss

The McClintock Security Series

Bound To Me

Return To Me

Steamy Standalones

Hollywood Dreams

Secrets and Lies